TH

A JAS NOVEL

LYDIA MICHAELS

BAILEY BROWN
PUBLISHING

The Best Man

A Jasper Falls Novel
Book 2

eBook ISBN: 978-1-7354677-5-7
Print ISBN: 978-1-7354677-6-4

Written by Lydia Michaels
Published by Bailey Brown Publishing
Cover Design by Lydia Michaels
Edited by Theresa Kohler; Oxford Comma Editing

Lydia Michaels
www.LydiaMichaelsBooks.com

Created with Vellum

For Theresa.
You are a glowing compass in the dark.
I'd be lost without you.

CHAPTER 1

"Drink! Drink! Drink! Drink!" The heavy pounding of many exuberant hands thumped down on the littered table, rattling empty bottles and jostling what was left of the cheesesteaks they ordered earlier.

Pat tipped back his shot and chugged hard, nearly choking himself on the thick taste of black beer and Irish cream. He was getting too old for this shit.

He slammed down his empty glass and roared like a champ, but his victorious cry was cut short by a belch that seemed to come from the deepest part of his soul. As a full-fledged medical doctor, he had it on good authority that his liver might not survive the next week. Tomorrow, he'd be back home in Jasper Falls, reunited with his crazy Irish family, celebrating the end of this chapter in his life as well as his brother's wedding. His insides would surely be fermented by then.

"Keep it down, Heaves!" his best friend, Jo, yelled, angering his sour stomach all the more with a hard smack on his back.

She'd called him Heaves ever since they were children,

when they broke into his parents' liquor cabinet. They drank so much it was a shock they hadn't ended up in the hospital. He'd spent the next several days dry heaving, and Jo spent the next fifteen years not letting him live it down.

"No more." He waved a hand over his glass as Dina attempted to refill it. "I have to drive in a few hours."

He squinted at the clock on the wall, debating if it was two or seven in the morning. He misplaced his glasses sometime around the cheesesteak feast. No one did cheesesteaks like Philadelphia, though it was up for debate who made the best sandwich. To commemorate his last night in the City of Brotherly Love, they ordered several from all the greats like Geno's, Pat's, Tony Luke's, and even Shank's. He definitely *did not* want to see his dinner return.

"We're gonna head home," Jeff said, his arm slung over Shay's shoulders as they staggered for a hug goodbye. "Don't be a stranger, man."

Pat kissed Shay's cheek and gave Jeff a thumping, manly hug. "I won't. Give me a call sometime next week and let me know how you make out at the animal rescue. Don't let Shay talk you into one of those little dogs people carry around in their purses."

Jeff laughed. "You got it."

"We should go, too," Dina said, nudging Brian, who had passed out on the table an hour ago.

The parade of goodbyes lasted several minutes, and soon their little apartment overlooking Broad was empty. Jo smiled at him, her dimpled cheeks the same as they were when they were children, mischievous and a great disguise to whatever was going on inside her always moving brain.

"What?" he asked, sensing she had something to get off her chest.

"Nothing." She shrugged. "I just can't believe you're leaving me."

"You always knew this would eventually happen."

"I know, but I got comfortable here. I like living with you."

He looped an arm over her shoulder and pressed an affectionate kiss on her cheek. "You know I'll be back."

"It won't be the same. I know how Jasper Falls works. Once you return, you get sucked in, and you never leave. You'll open your practice, be the town hero after you patch up a few scraped knees and stitch a busted face or two, then you'll forget all about your friends in the big-city."

He scrubbed a hand roughly over her short brown hair, mussing the stylish way she had it parted. "With that outlook, I might as well be living in a Norman Rockwell painting."

"You love that small town cheese-dick shit."

"True." His mouth hooked into a half smile.

After years of med school and finishing his residency, his life could *finally* begin. It seemed surreal that it was actually happening. His title and credibility had changed in a blink, yet he still felt like the same, unsure guy but with a lot more credentials and money. It almost felt fake or undeserved. He had a lot to prove, once he moved back home, and he wanted to make his family proud.

His mother was over the moon to claim one of her sons was a doctor. And since Doc Jones passed, their hometown was hurting for a replacement. He'd always dreamed of owning his own practice, something that usually took years to establish. But in a small town like Jasper Falls, where everyone knew everyone and people rarely trusted outsiders or big fancy hospitals, his practice would be a welcome addition.

He helped Jo gather plates and trash, only slightly stumbling toward the kitchen. "I'm going to hate you tomorrow. Whose idea was it to shoot Fireball?"

Jo laughed. "Yours."

"I'm an idiot."

"That's what I said. Where did you even find that bottle?"

He paused and scrunched his brow. "I think my brother gave it to me as a graduation present."

"From Penn?"

"No, from high school. Does alcohol expire?"

They finished cleaning up the table. There wasn't much to put away, being that most of his belongings were boxed up by the front door.

"Am I making a mistake?" he asked, staring at the pile of boxes marked *KEEP* to take home.

"No. You've always wanted this. And just think, you get to see Ryan every day. It'll be like old times."

He did miss his brother. "I can't believe he's getting married."

"To Maggie O'Malley no less. I never thought I'd see the day that an O'Malley married a Clooney."

"She's not, technically, an O'Malley." His brother's fiancée was an O'Malley by marriage. She was also the youngest widow in town—but she was about to marry into the biggest—and craziest—family in Jasper Falls.

"Everyone's getting married," Jo commented, plopping on the broken in couch, where Pat spent most of his nights after returning home from the hospital, too exhausted to find his bed.

He collapsed next to her and rested his head on her shoulder. "Not us."

She snorted. "I doubt I ever will."

He laced his fingers with hers, admiring the diamond ring on her right hand. It was the only feminine thing Jo owned. They found it stumbling home from the bar one night.

"You never know. Your soul mate could be out there somewhere."

"Oh, please." She lifted her hip and fished her phone out of her back pocket. "Speaking of which... Listen to this."

She opened her voicemail, flashing the screen with a list of calls from her mother and hit play.

"Josephine, it's impolite not to return someone's call, especially your mother's. I found a dress online that would look lovely with your eyes and hide your tattoos. I'm sending you the link. I think you should buy it for the wedding."

"A dress?"

"Wait," she said, scrolling down the voicemail page. "There's more."

"Josephine, I ran into Rosemary Clooney at McGinty's, and she said Ryan hasn't received your RSVP for the wedding yet. This reflects poorly on the family. I hope you've sent it by now."

She pursed her lips and narrowed her eyes at him. "You told Ryan I wasn't coming, right?"

"I mentioned it, but we still think you're going."

"Pat, I'm not going."

He lifted his chin at the phone, gesturing for her to play more.

She hit play on the next message. "Josephine, I spoke to Elise Wiseman today after mass, and she says that Tobin is looking for a date to the wedding. I gave her your number to pass along. Hopefully you answer the phone when he calls."

Pat scrunched his nose. "Tobin Wiseman?"

"I know. Even if I *was* into guys, I'd find him gross."

She played a few more messages, each one a testament to why she escaped her controlling, critical mother and ran away from her conservative family years ago. At least in Philly, she could be herself.

If he didn't know Dee and Rodger Cook, he'd advise her to *come out* to her family. It wasn't like the Cooks were all bad. Jo's older brother Garret was cool, and her younger brother Smith was fine, just at that post pubescent preadult indifferent stage. And Julie... Well, Julie was perfect, aside from her wretched taste in men.

But Jo's parents were a special kind of challenging. They lived in a bubble, got their news from unreliable sources, believed in actively repenting for their sins, and placed way too much emphasis on what others thought, especially when it came to their children.

He never understood why Jo earned such a difficult rap. She was no different than the others, but when it came to her mother, there seemed no pleasing the woman, especially where Jo was concerned. Maybe, on some level, Mrs. Cook already knew Jo's secrets. Sometimes, her expectations and criticism seemed more like an ongoing punishment than any twisted form of love.

Coming from a warm family like his, the Cooks' coldness chilled him to the bone, so he understood why Jo kept her sexuality to herself—at least where her family was concerned. Here, in the sanctuary of their little loft apartment, located in one of the most diverse cities in the world, Jo was *out* and proud.

He wished she felt confident enough to be herself at home. With the way things were, she'd never go back.

"I'll call her tomorrow and break the news that I'm not going. That should occupy my morning with a lengthy lecture, followed by an afternoon of undeserved guilt, and a long evening of drinking alone."

"Don't drink alone."

"But you're abandoning me." She pouted. "And Jeff and Shay will be busy with their new dog."

Together, they always had a partner they could count on, and he hated the idea of leaving her alone. He sat up and faced her. "Come home with me, Jo. Just for the wedding. I promise it won't be that bad. We can crash at my house most of the time."

She didn't immediately say no. "I do miss Rosemarie's cooking."

"It's not too late. I could call ahead and put in a menu request."

She hesitated, then shook her head. "No. I don't have the strength to deal with my mom. If I go home, she'll insist I take a date to the wedding. So help me God, if Tobin Wiseman tries to stick his tongue in my mouth, I'll be the new *Heaves*."

"What if there was a way to go home *and* get your mom off your back?"

"How?" She challenged him with heavy skepticism in her dark eyes.

The truth was, he had plenty of friends and family in Jasper Falls, but no one like Jo. Jo was his best friend. He wanted her there and couldn't imagine picking a new place to live without her skeptical input and dry cynicism guiding him away from every money pit. Plus, he wanted to see her sister, Julie—even if that meant having to stomach Lance.

"Tell your parents *we're* dating."

She burst into laughter, as if the idea were too hilarious to conceive.

He scowled. "It's not *that* unbelievable."

"No, I know, but..." She laughed harder, holding her stomach and falling back in a fit of unladylike snorts and cackles. "Me and you... I can't..." She wiped tears away from her eyes and blew out a breath. "Could you imagine?"

"Well, I clearly don't find it as difficult to imagine as you do!" He got up and went to the kitchen to take an aspirin.

"Pat, don't be mad!"

"I'm not mad. But I'll also never offer to be your boyfriend again."

"Oh, no. Whatever will I do without a fictional boyfriend?"

He narrowed his eyes and tossed back two white pills, chasing them with water. "You're mean."

"One of my best qualities."

"I guess I'll go to the wedding alone. Which is fine. I need to get laid."

"You're so cliché."

"Why? Because I want to hookup at my brother's wedding? Weddings are a great place to meet women."

"You know everyone on the guest list."

He shrugged. "Maggie could have some out-of-town relatives. I'm just looking for a one-nighter."

"Guys are so gross."

He shrugged. "If you feel so morally offended, you could prevent it by being my date."

"I'd be saving a woman a night of regrets and probably an STD test."

"Ouch." He laughed. "Come on, Jo, please…"

"Don't give me that look! You know it's my kryptonite!"

He fell beside her on the couch and did his best puppy dog stare. "If your mom thinks we're in a relationship, she'll stop trying to fix you up with every unclaimed penis in Jasper Falls."

"She'll know we're lying. Everyone knows we're just friends."

"I can be convincing. Before I decided to be a doctor, I toyed with improv. I could be the best boyfriend in the world, if the right girl ever gave me a shot."

Something knowing flashed in her eyes. "You know she'll be there with Lance."

His playful mood evaporated. "I know. It's expected."

Jo studied him for a long minute. It was no secret he'd been in love with her twin sister Julie his entire life. But, as a young boy, he'd been awkwardly shy and scrawny. He was the redhead with freckles that all the girls immediately lumped into the friend zone. By the time he filled out and got over his awkward adolescence, Julie had started dating Lance —the town douchebag. They'd been together ever since.

It was something they didn't discuss. Something he needed to put to rest if he ever wanted to move on and actually find a wife, preferably one who wanted him and was available. But he wasn't ready to retire the fantasy of Julie in his bed, arms, and future just yet—even if it was delusional and impossible.

"You'd be doing *me* a favor, actually. If we pretend we're dating, I won't have to come up with excuses about why I'm still single."

"Don't do that to me. Don't pull the favor card."

He shrugged. "Please?"

She groaned. "I hate you."

Sensing victory, he smiled. "Should we pack now or after we wake up?"

CHAPTER 2

The moment Pat turned the car onto Main Street his heart seemed to beat to a familiar tune. He was home.

"Wow," Jo said, staring out the passenger window. "When did they install new streetlights?"

"Sometime last spring." The old-fashioned lights gave the main road that small-town charm. It was an improvement from the hideous 1970's poles they had replaced.

Jo scowled. "Why does everything look so different? I've only been away for four years."

"A lot can happen in that time." Unlike Jo, whenever he heard of something happening in Jasper Falls or anywhere in Center County, he felt an ache of homesickness. He loved their little town and was happy to see it modernizing and growing—so long as it didn't get too big.

"Where did all these restaurants come from?"

He shook his head and scanned the lot at O'Malley's. "Wanna stop for a drink?" He spotted his cousin's hideous yellow Jeep.

"Let's do the parent thing first. Then I'll really want alcohol."

"It won't be *that* bad."

"Pat, I haven't been home for a birthday, holiday, or even a Sunday in four years. You know it won't be good."

He almost felt guilty for feeling excited to see his family, since Jo was experiencing the exact opposite. "We'll do your family first to get it over with."

He wondered when Julie would be coming to town. "Have you heard from your sister?"

Jo gave him *the look.* "No."

He glanced in the rearview mirror, checking his reflection and wondering if Julie would notice a change in him. He'd filled out over the last few years and finally found a decent hair stylist who could do something passable with his red waves. His new glasses helped a lot, too. He no longer looked like a kid from a 1950's comic strip. Plus, he was a doctor. Women supposedly liked that.

"Oh, God." Jo moaned as he pulled into the driveway behind her mother's Chrysler. It was the same van she drove when they were in high school. "How does everything else change, yet this place looks exactly the same?"

He shut off the engine, and they sat in silence, staring at the dated siding and faded lawn ornaments. Dee Cook didn't care for frills or fancy things, but she loved her some tacky lawn décor. He counted at least a dozen plastic geese.

"Are we getting out?"

"No." Jo's hands gripped the upholstered seat outside of her thighs. "Let's go back."

The front door opened, and Rodger Cook glowered at the car. "You didn't tell them you were coming, did you?"

"Now, why would I do that when surprising them is so much fun?"

He sighed and opened the door. "Hey, Mr. Cook."

"Patrick?"

"Yeah, it's me. And I brought a stowaway."

Mr. Cook scowled at the passenger door as Jo climbed out.

"Hey, Daddy."

"Josephine? What did you do to your hair? Your mother won't be happy about that."

"Good to see you, too." She glanced at Pat and gave him a panicked look, the same expression a hostage would make when they need to be rescued but couldn't speak without consequence.

"Well, are you coming in the house or just planning on standing in the driveway all day?"

"I hate you," she mumbled at Pat, then slammed the door. "We're coming."

Pat followed her into the unfashionable living room where dated school photos filled a variety of mismatched frames. In the back room, where the Cooks typically watched television—mostly televised church services—they found Mrs. Cook.

"Our daughter's home," Mr. Cook announced.

"Julie?" Mrs. Cook's expression lifted, then twisted with disappointment, when she saw Jo. "What have you done to your beautiful hair?"

"Hi, Mom." Jo leaned down and kissed her mother's gaping face.

"It's so short. You look like a boy!"

"How are you, Mrs. Cook?" Pat asked, trying to take some of the attention off Jo. "Is that a new afghan you're working on?"

She glanced down at her crochet needle and yarn. "They're place mats. I'm making them for your brother and Maggie as a wedding present."

They were hideous. "I hope I can be there when you give them to him."

"I suppose." She turned her cold stare back to Jo. "I hope you brought something decent to wear to the wedding. Jeans are unacceptable." Her gaze dropped to the tattered pair only slightly covering Jo's legs. "Did you at least have the courtesy to tell them you were coming?"

The front door opened, and Pat turned, grinning widely at the sight of Jo's two brothers. "Hey, Garret. Smith."

Smith, Jo's younger brother, waved and dashed up the steps, hardly acknowledging his sister or parents. Garret shook his hand. "Clooney, good to see you. I heard you're all done school now."

"Finished my residency this week."

"That's great, man." He turned his attention to his sister. "And who is this bombshell? This couldn't possibly be my baby sister."

"Hey, Garret." Her entire demeanor had been tense since they arrived, but Garret wasn't having any of it.

He swept her up in a back cracking hug and shook her, until she laughed and begged to be put down. "Welcome home, sis."

"Thanks, but we can't stay long."

Her mother tsked. "You just got here."

"Pat hasn't seen his family yet."

"So, let him go. You're not connected at the hip. Besides, I want you to give that Tobin a call—"

"Tobin Wiseman?" Garret asked, repeating Pat's look of concern from the day before. "What's she gotta call him for?"

"Garret, you stay out of it. Your sister's been single too long. It's beginning to look suspicious—"

"Mom, I'm not calling Tobin—"

"Don't sass me, Josephine. You need a date for the wedding."

That wasn't at all true, but Mrs. Cook always had her own weird book of rules she seemed to follow.

"Actually…" Pat cleared his throat. "Jo's going to the wedding with me."

"You?" Mrs. Cook's response was a bit of an ego crusher. "That won't work at all. She needs to go with an actual date."

"Pat is my date, Mom."

"Oh, please. Do I look like I was born yesterday?"

"It's true." Jo wrung her hands, and he frowned wondering what she was doing with her fingers and then his eyes widened as he noticed she'd switched the diamond ring to her left ring finger. "As a matter of fact, we're getting married."

"What?" Garret looked as if they just claimed the sky was yellow and two plus two was nine.

Mr. and Mrs. Cook gaped at them. Mrs. Cook broke the silence first. "And this is how you tell us? Most people call or even write! What did we ever do to deserve such inconsideration from you?"

Jo smiled, and for once, Pat suspected she was suffering actual joy at her mother's disappointment. "Aren't you happy for us?" She hooked her arm through his and yanked him closer.

Garret scowled at him, but he didn't know what to say. Pat agreed to pretend he and Jo were dating for a week. But marriage or being a fake fiancé was never on the table.

Mrs. Cook rolled her eyes. "No one likes a thunder stealer, Josephine. You'll have your wedding, but this week's about Ryan and Maggie."

Jo laughed without humor. "Unbelievable. You could find the negative in anything I do."

"This isn't about you!" her mother shrilled. In a huff, she rose from her recliner, leaving a tangle of yarn in her wake, and stomped out of the room.

Jo looked at her father expectantly. "Daddy?"

He sighed. "You'll have to wait until after your sister's wedding. She got engaged first, and I'm not paying for two at a time."

Pat's stare jerked to Jo and his heart sank as he recognized the apology in her eyes. She knew. She knew and she didn't tell him. "Julie's engaged?"

Her apologetic eyes said it all. She'd kept this secret from him for a while.

Considering that he was supposed to be engaged to Jo, he should have done more to hide his shock. But part of him always believed Julie would eventually snap out of it and realize what an ass Lance was. He never actually expected her to marry the jerk.

And the longer Garrett watched him, the more transparent Pat felt. Rubbing the back of his neck, he glanced at Jo. "We should really get going. My mom's expecting us."

CHAPTER 3

"You missed the turn to your house."

"I know." Pat pulled into the parking lot of O'Malley's and slammed the car in park. "Too far, Jo!"

"I'm sorry! She was saying so many hurtful things, and I wanted to hurl something back at her."

"I'm not talking about that. I'm talking about Julie! How long have you known?"

Her brows pulled tight. "He proposed about four months ago."

"What the hell? We don't lie to each other—ever. How could you keep this from me?"

"Well, look at you! You're a mess. I didn't want to hurt you."

"I'm not a mess!"

"Pat." She flipped down the visor, and his reflection flashed before his eyes. His complexion was blotchy and his skin wore a sheen of sweat. In a softer voice, she said, "I know you love her, but this isn't healthy. People move on. We have to let them."

His gaze dropped to his lap. "I just… I just thought I'd eventually have a shot."

"I know." The weight of her hand rested gently on his shoulder. "Me, too."

He sighed. "I didn't grasp how much I actually believed it would eventually happen, until I realized it wouldn't. She's *actually* going to marry him."

"Did you really believe she wouldn't? I mean, she moved to Maryland with him years ago. I don't think she ever planned on returning to Jasper Falls."

But in his head, she always came home. They had a charming little house on the outskirts of town and three little kids, all with pale blonde hair, like their mother, and his blue eyes. The youngest daughter would be sweet and precocious like Julie, the oldest would be brave and brazen like Jo, and the boy would be a Clooney through and through.

He needed help. In his head, he even had a list of names for their fake chocolate lab.

Grabbing the keys from the ignition, he shoved open the door. "I need a beer."

Stepping into the dimly lit bar brought about a rush of nostalgia that was cut short by the unfamiliar changes in the lighting and painted walls. He frowned, noting the obvious improvement but rejecting it on principle.

"Okay, way too much shit's changing," Jo said, taking the words right out of his mouth.

O'Malley's had always been owned by his family. But last winter, they sold it to his future sister-in-law and her sister—Peppin or Paris or something. He scanned the bar and assumed that was her.

"What do you want to drink?"

"Order me something from five years ago so we can reverse the hallucination I'm having," Jo murmured. "Since when does O'Malley's put out candles and flowers?"

"Be nice." He approached the bar. "Hey… Pep…per…aris."

The bartender frowned at him. "Are you having a stroke?"

His face flushed with embarrassment. "I'm sorry, I forget your name."

"Have we met?"

Nothing like being forgettable. "I'm Ryan's brother, Patrick."

"Oh, Patrick! Now I remember you!" She laughed. "The name's Perrin."

Perrin. He needed to remember that. "Is Maggie around?"

"No, she and Ryan had to do a cake tasting in town. What can I get you?"

He ordered two beers and heard a screech from the pool tables in the back. A split second later, he was being attacked by a redheaded devil.

"You're home!" His cousin Sheilagh tackled him like a crazed ape loose at the zoo, then sprung off his back and clobbered Jo with hugs and kisses. "Oh, my God, I *love* your hair! City life totally agrees with you! And—" She snatched Jo's left hand in an unbreakable grip. "What the holy hell is this?"

Jo pressed her lips tight in a cheeky smirk and flashed her dimples. "I'm getting married."

"You are? To who?"

Jo looked over Sheilagh's shoulder, and his cousin turned to follow her stare, looking right through him. She turned back to Jo. "Who is it?"

Jo laughed. "It's Patrick."

"No, seriously, who is it?"

"Well, my self-esteem's about shot for the day," he muttered, then waved Perrin closer. "Can I get a shot of Tully with my beer?"

"You got it."

The bartender stepped away and Sheilagh frowned. "What's the punch line?"

"There isn't one. Pat and I are getting married."

"No, you're not."

His shot arrived and he tossed it back. Sheilagh wasn't the most tactful person, but she also wasn't stupid. "Just tell her."

But Jo was having too much fun messing with her. "We're in love."

"Nope. Not buying it," Sheilagh snapped. "First, it's Pat—"

"Thanks, cuz."

"Second, he's serving frank and beans, and last I checked, you were only ordering tacos."

"Classy." He sipped his beer.

"And third, no offense, but he's been completely obsessed with your sister, since she shared her pudding cup with him in Mrs. Kreb's class."

And that was his limit. He pointed to the empty glass. "Another shot."

"You got it." At least Perrin was on her game.

Jo shook her head. "Ix-nay on the *Ulie-Jay*."

"Tell me the truth."

"Fine, Pat bribed me to come home by promising to be my boyfriend, so my mom would stop trying to fix me up with all her church friends' sons. I thought this would be more fun."

"Oh my God, how did she take it?"

"Not well. It was great!"

Sheilagh's eyes widened. "You guys are going to have to keep this up all week with the way news travels in this town."

"It'll never work." His other shot was delivered and he pushed a few dollars forward on the bar. "Too many people know we're just friends. And anyone who actually knows you knows I'm not your type." Was he anyone's type?

"I don't know," Sheilagh debated. "I think it's believable. I mean, friends to lovers is a popular pattern. Plenty of people marry their best friend."

Was Lance Julie's best friend? What did they talk about? What could she possibly have in common with that guy? Certainly not enough to spend the rest of her life with him. Good thing the whiskey was kicking in.

"Let's test it out."

"Wait. What?" Before Pat could stop her, Sheilagh plugged two fingers into her mouth and let out a long, sharp whistle.

Sue popped her head out of the kitchen and smiled. "Pat!"

"You're both evil," he grumbled.

Sue had been a bartender at O'Malley's for years. She knew all the latest town gossip and had a talent for sniffing out bullshit.

Pat greeted her with a hug, and Jo did the same. "Josephine! I didn't know you were coming home, too."

Jo shrugged. "I figured I'd make a quick appearance. Besides, we have some news." She waved her fingers, flashing the diamond ring.

Sue gasped and examined the ring. "Dear Lord, is that what sunk the Titanic?"

"It's gorgeous, isn't it? Pat did a great job picking it out."

Sue did a double take and gaped at them with a wide smile. "You did this?"

He might as well play along. "Guilty."

"Well, it's about time. I mean, I heard you two were living together, but I just assumed it was business as usual. No one told me you were actually gettin' busy out there in the city. Congratulations!"

Sheilagh smirked and winked. If they could fool Sue, they could fool anyone. Besides Sheilagh, no one really knew Jo dated women.

They had a celebratory round of drinks, and soon Maggie and Ryan arrived. Pat was tipsy enough to actually play into the lie, and it felt nice to pretend for a minute. But when his brother got the news and gave him that skeptical look, he knew they were caught. It wasn't that Ryan knew Jo was gay but that he'd suffered through countless conversations about Julie. When Pat was younger, he could spend hours obsessing over one of her eyelashes alone.

Ryan used to tease them, accusing Jo of being in love with him, but Pat had always been adamant that they were only friends. That could, of course, change. But the real giveaway was that Pat hadn't mentioned proposing to his brother. Aside from Sheilagh and Jo, Ryan was his best friend and greatest confidant. He confided in him about everything—especially the big, life-altering decisions.

His brother's hand slapped onto his shoulder in a hard grip disguised as a gesture to congratulate him, and the next thing Pat knew, he was being steered into the back of the bar.

"Mind telling me what the hell's going on?"

"Uh..."

"Look, Pat, I think it's great that you and Jo finally figured things out. But if I did something to you or gave you a reason to believe I wouldn't be happy for you—"

"Ry, no, that's not it at all."

"You're sure? Because you can be honest with me. I think this is great."

His brother's sincere trust in him stunned him. He had to tell him. "Ry..."

"There you are." Maggie appeared and smiled up at Pat. "I'm so happy for you, Patrick."

He didn't really know his brother's fiancée. She was quiet and sort of shy. He wondered if she would always be there now, like for awkward confessions intended only for his older brother. He'd rather explain things in private.

"Hey, Maggie. How was the cake tasting?"

"Oh, man," Ryan jumped in. "Did you know guys get a groom's cake?"

"A what?"

"A cake, just for the groom."

As his brother went on and on describing the various cakes and fillings, he noted how relaxed and excited he seemed. Pat couldn't recall a time he ever saw him so happy. The thought of disturbing that happiness, in any way, felt like a crime.

When his cousin Luke got to the bar, Ryan was all too excited to share the news. And in a family like theirs, news had a way of traveling quickly. It wasn't long before his phone was ringing.

"I have to take this. It's my dad." Pat covered his ear and stepped away from the bar. "We got tied up, Dad, but we'll be there soon."

"Patrick, you better get here *now.* Your mother just got a call from Aunt Maureen with some news and—"

"Shit."

"Yup. And you're deep in it."

Of course, his cousins would waste no time with fresh gossip. And once any new information got to his Aunt Maureen, it ultimately reached his mother's ears in under a minute. "Okay. We're on our way."

"Good. And Pat?"

"Yeah, Dad?"

"Congratulations."

He hesitated, wondering why he ever thought to go along with Jo's stupid joke. "Thanks, Dad."

~

WHEN THEY REACHED HIS PARENTS' house, his mother squealed with excitement, gobbling Jo into a full body hug.

"Oh, I just knew it! I knew one day you two would fall in love. I went from having no daughters to getting two all in one year!"

"Uh, Mum, it's still early."

Her euphoric expression morphed into something cold and accusing. "Well, it can't be too early, because the entire clan of your cousins already knew—*before* your own mother."

He shut his eyes, wondering how long it would take to live this down. Probably as long as her disappointment, once she found out the whole engagement was a sham. "I'm fucked."

"What's that?" his father asked, leaning in to better hear him.

"I said I'm hungry." He headed into the kitchen and came up short when he found Tristan rummaging through the fridge. "Hey, I didn't know you were here."

"Been here all day trying to fix that damn boiler. Your dad refuses to get a new one. It squeals all day when it runs and burns through fuel twice as fast as the newer models."

"What do you expect? It's seventy years old."

He shut the fridge and gave Pat an appraising look. "I hear congratulations are in order." There was no inflection to his voice.

Tristan had gone to college with Ryan. After they graduated, he moved into their house as a sort of surrogate brother from another mother. He'd since moved out and married Luke, but he still came home to fix things here and there.

"Why are you looking at me like that?"

Tristan shrugged. "I just find it strange."

"What?"

"I always assumed you weren't Jo's type."

He was getting tired of hearing how he didn't qualify as husband material. "Does anyone really have a *type* these days?"

Tristan arched a brow. "Girls like Jo do."

Something flashed in his eyes, and a shiver of paranoia raced up his spine. Did Tristan know Jo was gay? He was almost certain she never told him, but he'd have to double-check. If he knew, they'd all eventually know, which was inevitable anyway because this whole thing had spun drastically out of control.

His mum was so happy for them. This was going to crush her. He should come clean now before more people found out.

"Hey, you okay?"

"What?" He blinked and realized Tristan was still staring at him. "Yeah. I'm fine. I just need some air." He pushed past Tristan, escaping out the back door.

CHAPTER 4

Julie gripped the steering wheel of her Mercedes and stared through the windshield at her unchanged childhood home. The vision seemed to comfort, like a noose around her neck. Returning to Jasper Falls for Ryan Clooney's wedding was not quite the homecoming she expected. But it was absolutely the escape she needed.

Her gaze shifted to the box of belongings resting on the passenger seat. It certainly wasn't enough to represent a life. But it was all she could afford to bring with her.

Leaving Lance was less about the possessions she could get out the door and more about the shreds of dignity she could maintain through the exit. He dismantled her so carefully over such a long period of time, she forgot how to trust herself.

Even now, more than a hundred miles away from him, she felt like a ticking time bomb. At any second, her whole world could explode into another mess. No warning. No sense of preparation. Just the overwhelming feeling that she had lost control of everything.

Was she making a mistake? A knot formed in her stomach as her grip tightened on the wheel. Should she go back?

She never knew if she was overreacting or doing the right thing anymore. Was she the victim of gaslighting or was she truly just crazy?

Lance had her thinking so screwed up, simple tasks like folding laundry could make her anxious. She was burnt out from trying not to mess up, but according to him, she did very little right.

"You don't listen. You never listen. You always just hear what you want to hear." Similar accusations played on a loop in her head, taunting her and making her question her sanity.

She could still see that condescending look in his eye, the one that made her feel foolish and crazy. He claimed he never said he'd come home for the wedding, but she swore they had a conversation about just that.

"Julie, I said it would be nice to take a trip home for Ryan's wedding, not that I would go. Some of us have work."

Of course, he never missed the chance to jab at her unemployment. It was her decision to leave her job, but he'd contributed to that choice by making her feel less competent than others.

Inadequacy went both ways when it came to her career. He said he loved having her home to take care of things but often made comments that implied he thought less of her for not working outside of the house.

"You really have to listen better, Julie. Sometimes I think you write these narratives in your head and totally disregard reality."

Yet, when they discussed the wedding, he'd asked her to make sure his suit was pressed, and she'd taken care of it the next day.

"We RSVP'd," she'd reminded him, only to receive another look that told her she'd overreached.

"That's on you. If we ever sincerely discussed this, I would have

checked my calendar. I'm not like you. I can't just flake out on my obligations."

"Lance... You did check your calendar. This was several months ago. Remember?"

"No, and my memory is spot on. I don't know why you want to go anyway. No one in Jasper Falls cares about seeing you. Your sister won't be there. Why would you even bother making the drive?"

For days, she'd debated calling the Clooneys and making up an excuse, maybe even lying and saying she and Lance had the flu. But in the end, she wanted to see Ryan get married.

True, Jo wouldn't be there. She left Jasper Falls four years ago and never looked back, but Pat would definitely be at his brother's wedding. Remembering her old friends brought about a sense of nostalgic simplicity, something she really had been longing for lately—especially when she thought of Patrick.

Her heart pinched with regret. Julie always believed she and her twin sister would never live far apart, but a few years ago Jo up and moved to Philadelphia, completely abandoning their life in Jasper Falls to go live with Pat.

The three of them had always been close. She and Jo were linked by their sibling bond, and Pat, well, she supposed it was never about her, after all, and Jo was the one he favored most.

As they grew older and Julie started dating, she and Patrick grew apart, yet he and Jo remained tight. Pat had stopped acting silly with Julie and she often envied the ease Jo kept with him, laughing at inside jokes and sharing experiences Julie hadn't been invited to join.

Without Jo, Julie didn't see a reason to stay in Jasper Falls. Lance's job was transferring him to Maryland. It made the best sense for her to follow him.

Her head dropped back to the headrest, and she shut her eyes, exhausted from the sheer thought of her life. She hadn't prepared her family for her return. They didn't know this trip home might be a permanent one.

A tear slowly rolled from the corner of her eye as a sense of failure and embarrassment cocooned her. Her thumb rotated the engagement ring on her finger. She couldn't bring herself to take it off, because she still wasn't convinced this was the right move.

Her mind snapped into a sharp reprimand. This absolutely was the right decision. She needed to get out of that toxic environment. But she had so much to consider.

When narcissists weren't being nasty, they were extremely charming, and part of her still loved Lance. Their love was real and passionate and intense. She hadn't imagined that part.

"You put way more into your family than they ever put into you, Julie. Don't you think Jo would have stuck around if she was that close to you? I'll never leave you. I'm your family."

She thought about the multiple audiobooks on her phone, the ones she'd been secretly listening to over the past few months. When her self-esteem had hit rock bottom, she needed to figure out what was going on with her. Audiobooks seemed the only therapy she could access without drawing unwanted attention from Lance, who she'd determined was a great source of her low moods.

"Do you like this dress?"

"Yeah, it's sexy. But you gotta watch your figure. Don't become one of those women who get comfortable and let themselves go. When's the last time you used the gym?"

Lance's honesty always felt like something she could trust. She didn't want a partner who lied. She wanted a friend who trusted their relationship enough to always give her the truth. Whether she had food in her teeth or if she was on the wrong side of a disagreement, she always wanted to know.

"I promise I'll always be honest with you. That's what true love is."

But the problem with constant honesty was that he never let her forget her character flaws. He didn't focus on them, but he certainly had a way of reminding her they were there, like the way an athlete occasionally stops to check their pulse.

Over time, that steady barrage of honest feedback turned her into a less than honest person. She kept secrets and hid shameful parts of herself to avoid criticism. But he even had a gift for somehow making compliments hurt.

"I'm sure there are better qualified candidates for the job, but you're pretty. Companies want a good face. Maintain your looks and no one will notice what you lack."

Lance's opinions became the highest authority.

"Why would you do that that way? Didn't anyone ever teach you..."

She wasted hours doubting and second guessing herself, not wanting to screw anything up. Her days passed in a strange confusion. Eventually, she feared making any decisions at all.

Lance had always been so confident and sure of himself. Even when he was wrong, he seemed so convincingly right, it just felt safer to trust him.

He was the success story. *He* was the obvious decision-maker. Sometimes she wondered why a guy like Lance would ever be with a girl like her.

I'm sorry seemed a regular phrase out of her mouth but rightfully so, as she was always screwing something up. It got to the point where she would do almost anything to avoid any sort of confrontation or failure, even the mildest sort.

The pressure was paralyzing. If she remained completely

still and didn't make any waves, she couldn't mess up. Her life was passing in neutral. And soon, she lost complete touch with the girl she once was.

The more agreeable she became, the more control Lance assumed. And when she did object, she quickly regretted saying anything at all, as it was just another opening for criticism.

"You're too sensitive."

Was she? It sometimes felt like she might be. She was always overthinking and doubting herself.

She'd been seeing a chiropractor and massage therapist for the last month. Because her tension had gotten so bad, she suffered a persistent crick in her neck and chronic headaches.

The light bulb moment came when she read there was no escaping through the entrance when trying to leave a relationship with a gaslighter, because their insidious tampering changed a person's perception of reality until everything seemed turned around and the victim felt lost.

She was lost. And it killed her to realize that meant she was a victim. But she wasn't crazy. Deep down she knew this.

He'd done such a thorough job of rewriting her behaviors and thoughts that he rarely had to say anything at all. She'd become an automatically-charged weapon—blaming, doubting, and judging herself for him in his absence. He turned *her* into her worst critic, so he could remain the shining hero. It was, without a doubt, the greatest mindfuck she'd ever known.

He was a manipulative monster hiding beneath the mask of a beautiful charmer. She wasn't even sure how he did it. The devotion it must take to chip away at a sane person until they feel completely insane… Lance had been controlling the narrative for so long, she no longer felt like the author of her own life.

Her phone buzzed on the dashboard, and she didn't need to look to know it was him. He'd filled up her voicemail a hundred miles ago.

Funny, when she announced she was leaving him, she was nothing but a waste and she'd never find someone who loved her as much as him again. No one would want her… But now, he wanted her back.

If she was so terrible, why would he care if she left?

The books said this whiplash reaction often happened because a narcissist saw others as toys. For years, she acted as a ricochet point for Lance to sound off his self-inflating ideas. She'd listen and agree and be the perfect audience for his egotistical masturbation. He said *she* needed *him,* but really, it was *he* who needed *her.*

She didn't care if he moved on. But, in a strange way, she did. It was like he was two people in one, the charmer and the monster. She hated the monster. But the charmer…

It hurt her stomach to think of him touching someone else or loving someone else. Why couldn't he have stayed the charmer and always been nice? Why wasn't she enough—

No! That was her self-blaming again. She *was* enough. Their issues were the result of a deficiency in him. He was a charmer, but he was also an abuser, and she needed to remember that.

When she left, he was so out of his mind enraged by the thought that someone like her could reject someone as incredible as him. He flung the most hurtful diatribe at her, attacking her body, her intelligence, her sexual performance. But most hurtful of all, he attacked her relationships with others—making her wonder if anyone would ever want her, to a point that she even doubted her family's love.

"Too late to go back now," she muttered, glancing at the screen of her phone where several notifications waited.

She swiped the device and quickly skimmed his texts, a

long jumble of apologies, begging, and attacking slurred into one. He was so off-kilter by their break up he'd already made his rounds with their mutual friends, trying to poison the waters to make sure she would come out the villain.

The books all said to expect a break up to be brutal and sudden, mentioning the necessity of getting out quickly. They suggested that several things may need to be left behind, but they weren't just referencing possessions. They meant friendships, too.

She'd have to disentangle her life from his completely, if she truly wanted to be finished with him. Eventually, he'd stop calling. He'd move on, because once she stopped feeding his ego, he'd feel desperate for a new audience and find someone else to stroke him.

This break up wasn't about *her.* Their relationship was never about *her.* Everything a narcissist did, they did for themselves. People were chosen, not for who they were, but for what they could provide.

It would be nice to find someone who actually valued *her.* But she was a long way from dating. Right now, she needed a safe place to think and heal, a place where she could process and recover and teach herself how to make decisions again.

There was no place safer than Jasper Falls.

CHAPTER 5

"Oh, will you look at that?" Pat's restful peace shifted at the rasp of his mother's voice. "Like two wee pups, curled up together to keep warm. Remember when we used to cuddle like that, Liam?"

His father's grumbled reply had Pat cracking open an eyelid. He should have known better than to pass out on the sectional with Jo last night. He spotted his mother sitting across from him on her recliner, watching them sleep.

She grinned and sipped her tea, holding the mug in two hands as the steam curled her faded red hair. "Mornin' Patrick."

"Do you have to watch me sleep, Mum?"

"I carried you for nearly a year, gave up my youthful figure, and nursed you 'til my nipples were sore. If I gain the slightest comfort from watching my baby sleep, I'll do it without censure."

He groaned and rolled his eyes, turning to face the back of the sofa and disturbing Jo.

"Why are your knees so boney?"

"Good morning, Josephine," his mother greeted.

"Morning, Mrs. Clooney."

"Oh, now, we won't be havin' any more of that, love. You call me Rose—or Mum."

Reality came hurtling back to him and he internally winced at the reminder that they were living a lie. Maybe now was the time to come clean, before his mother did something crazy like booked the church.

"I've made an appointment for you with the realtor, Patrick. We have to be in town in an hour."

He frowned and twisted to face his mother again. "What realtor?"

"The young woman who took over at the Perkin's agency. She has a simple name like Ruth or Peg. You know me with names. Anyway, I set it up because she's very busy, you see? And as much as I love having you back home, these things take time. I'm not planning to support one of those college-graduate sons who pass off their debt to their parents. I watch the news."

"Mum, what the hell are you talking about? I paid off most of my debt during my residency."

"Even still. I've promised the town a doctor, and you can't practice medicine out of our house. The appointment's at ten. Jo, I assume you'll want a say in this. After all, you'll be living wherever Patrick lives."

"Uh..."

His glare drilled into Jo's guilty stare, but she said nothing. "Mum, we have to tell you something."

"What is it, dear?"

"We—"

"Want to find a place closer to town," Jo interrupted. He was going to murder her. "An office with an apartment on top. That's enough for now."

"Like a starter home? That's probably wise. I should call Connie and let her know, so she can check the listings. I had assumed you'd want a house."

"Who's Connie?"

His mother was already moving toward the phone. "The realtor. Pay attention, Patrick."

She disappeared into the kitchen, and he looked to his father, who was doing a puzzle in a book. "Did she not say the realtor's name was Peg or Ruth?"

Without lifting his gaze, his father made a mark in the book with a filed down pencil and said, "I stopped listening twenty years ago, Pat. Better do what she asked and get dressed."

He took a quick shower and found Jo waiting on his bed. She'd helped herself to one of his flannels and fixed her hair. He scowled at her. "Why didn't you let me tell her? This is getting out of hand."

"She just seemed so happy to have me. She told me to call her Mum."

He got it. Jo's mom treated her like a burden most days, always trying to fit her into a mold that Jo would never fit, but this was not going to end well. That reminded him...

"Does Tristan know you're a lesbian?"

"I never told him, but probably. I pegged him for liking guys way before he and Luke came out."

"You did?" Another thing she never told him.

"It was just a feeling."

"Well, I think he knows we're lying."

"I'm not surprised about Tristan. People talk. Maybe Sheilagh told him."

He stepped into jeans and pulled on a T-shirt. "We *need* to tell my mom we're lying. She's going to start picking out china patterns and make me buy an excessively large house for the wife and family I'm not going to have." At least not yet.

"That's why I said we want an apartment. I know you don't want a house yet."

It was a little disturbing how quick on her feet she was with the lies. He grabbed his keys and stuffed them into his pocket. "We're telling her. Let's go."

They met with the realtor, whose name happened to be Darlene, and visited several different properties. He wasn't emotionally prepared for house hunting, but he made the best of it.

"Maggie's house is still on the market. You and Ryan could be neighbors."

"No. I don't want a house, Mum."

"But, eventually, you'll start a family. Don't you want children, Jo?"

Jo smiled and opened a closet, peeking into the empty space. "This place has a smell. What is that? It's like a cross between popcorn and kerosene."

His mother took a big sniff of the closet. "Oh, that smells like rotten eggs."

"I don't like the location of this place anyway. What's next?" They had to move this along. He promised Ryan he'd step into his role as best man and help him today.

"I have a small storefront at the end of Main Street. It's only fifteen hundred square feet on each floor—"

"Perfect," Pat said. "Let's go there."

They drove to the end of Main Street, and he immediately remembered the store as the old Second Chance Bookshop. It had a storage area in the back and a private entrance leading to the second floor. The floorplan was open, but there was the potential for walls. He could see a waiting room, a small office, enough storage space for files and a front desk, and two small patient rooms. It was tight but the best he'd seen so far.

"What's the listing price on this one?"

Darlene handed him the information page. His mother frowned and examined the run down cabinetry in the back.

"Patrick, this isn't at all what I was picturing."

Reviewing the sheet, he said, "We would renovate, Mum. All that would get gutted and replaced." The price was good. It left plenty of room for construction costs. "Let's see the upstairs."

The upstairs was what the realtor called *cozy* in order to avoid words like small or cramped. Since it was connected to another store, there were only windows on the front, back, and south facing wall, letting in minimal light. But there was a roof area he could see setting up with a barbeque and tiki bar. All in all, it was perfect.

"Can I come back? I'd like to show my brother." Ryan's opinion always helped when it came to big decisions.

"I'll leave you the lockbox code, so you can take a second look. It's been sitting a while, so you have time."

"Oh, Patrick, I just don't know." His mother didn't approve—and her disapproval could be brutal, because she was never the sort to sit silently by and watch her children make mistakes, even when they weren't mistakes. "How will you get furniture up such a narrow staircase? The lack of light could cause seasonal depression. And the kitchen's hardly a kitchen at all. How will you entertain?"

"Who am I entertaining, Mum? This is fine."

"I like it," Jo chimed in. "It's actually pretty perfect."

Something strange happened, something he never witnessed before. At Jo's opposing opinion, his mother...bit her tongue. What was this witchcraft?

"Well," his mother responded hesitantly. "Far be it for me

to be one of those intrusive mothers-in-law. You'll be the one having to make it a home."

The thought of Jo being any sort of apron-wearing homemaker made him chuckle. And he knew such an idea would make her twitch, so he went with it.

Slinging his arm over her shoulder, he smiled. "Yeah, babe. Just think, you'll be over there cooking me dinner and setting the table. We can get one of those electric fireplaces, and I could put my feet up over here by the window, in my favorite chair, while you fetch me a martini and the remote, maybe even treat me to a little foot rub. And we'll live happily ever after."

She smiled with gritted teeth. "Sounds *lovely.*"

His mother gave them a strange look. "I can teach you a few things wives should know."

He swallowed a laugh. "Wow, Mum, that's really generous of you. Jo was just saying she wished she could be more domestic. She really has an affinity for the way things used to be. You can help her find her inner Donna Reed."

He ignored the way Jo's nails dug into his arm. She could stop this at any time. But if she was sticking to the lie, he was going to make her work for it.

Jo's phone pinged and she pulled it from her back pocket. "Julie's here."

"Julie?" All thoughts of house hunting derailed as his mind filled with images of the woman he loved. God, he had to stop torturing himself. "When did she get here?"

"Last night. She didn't realize I was in town. She wants to see me."

"Let's go." He sounded way too eager.

"What about the other listings?" his mother asked.

He checked his watch. It was only eleven. He told Ryan he'd be by around noon. If he wanted to see Julie, he needed to wrap this up. "I like this place."

"Patrick, you need to see all your options."

"Can we meet again later this week?" he asked the realtor.

"Sure, my schedule's pretty open." Of course, it was. Things were only ever urgent in his mother's mind.

"Great. I'll give you a call." He was already walking toward the door, and Jo was rolling her eyes.

She kept her mouth shut, until they dropped off his mother. As soon as they were alone in the car, she let him have it.

"I swear you'd chew off your own arm to get to a girl who's not at all available to you, Pat. Why do you do this to yourself?"

"I was doing it for you. You said she needed to see you."

"Bullshit. You're using me as an excuse."

He didn't deny it. "I haven't seen her in over a year."

She sighed. "She's engaged."

"Well, according to the rest of Jasper Falls so are we. She's my friend."

"Really? When was the last time you called her?"

"Why do you care?"

"Because I don't want to see you get hurt. This is like self-masochism. Every time there's a holiday or anything, you obsess over seeing her and then you mope around the rest of the time, because *news flash,* she's still with Lance."

He beeped at a car waiting at a green light. "Go!" The car moved, and he felt Jo's stare burning into him. "Stop looking at me like that."

He knew he was acting like an obsessed stalker. He didn't want to hear her laundry list of reasons about how unhealthy his fixation with Julie was. He got it. He suffered it every day for the last twenty plus years. He'd eventually get over her, but right now, he needed to concentrate and prepare himself, because where Julie was, Lance was, and he *hated* seeing that arrogant douchebag.

He spotted Julie's car the instant they turned onto Jo's street. It was probably the only Mercedes within a fifty mile radius of Jasper Falls, and while he liked the idea of Julie living a luxurious life, he hated the idea of a guy like Lance supplying it. Last he heard, she gave up her job, which was a shame because Julie had always been sharp as hell.

He parked the car and took a moment to catch his breath. Why was he breathing so heavily?

"You gonna be okay?"

"I'm fine," he snapped. "Sorry."

The judgement in Jo's stare shifted to sympathy. "My sister would have been the luckiest girl in the world, if she could have just given you a chance."

He grinned, understanding her meaning. No one would ever love Julie as deeply as him. He saw her imperfections but found them so innocent and human, they only added to her beauty. He loved her vulnerability, her determination, her empathy for others, and the way she could solve almost any problem, if she set her mind to it. The only unforgivable flaw she had was her atrocious taste in men. But he couldn't blame her for being devoted to Lance. She was loyal to a fault.

"Ready?"

He sighed. "Yeah."

Jo was right, this was a form of masochism. He took no pleasure from seeing Julie with Lance, yet he suffered through it every chance he got.

They walked up the path, as if traversing to the gallows. Every faded, plastic goose judging him harshly along the way.

"Hello?"

"Josephine? Where have you been?" her mother called from the back room. He could hear the morning church service playing on the television.

"I slept at Pat's."

They entered the back den, and his heart spiked and plummeted. Julie sat cross-legged on the love seat, in a faded Bears sweatshirt and plaid pajama pants. Her face was scrubbed clean, looking not a day past sixteen, and her pale blonde hair was twisted up in a messy knot on her head. Although she and Jo were twins, they were far from identical. Jo was dark and devious, but Julie was light and softness, a fresh fallen bed of snow on a perfect winter day.

"Patrick," she said affectionately with a delicate smile, and his heartbeat tripled at the sound of his name on her lips.

"Julie."

Her gaze shifted to Jo and her smile bloomed. Only then did he notice the bags under her eyes, the fragility of her posture, and the way her nails were bitten down to nubs. Something wasn't right. Where was Lance?

Jo joined her sister on the sofa and hugged her.

"You said you weren't coming." Julie brushed her fingers through Jo's dark hair. "I love this. And…" She frowned, her hand lifting Jo's so she could examine the ring. "So, it's true?" His stomach cramped as Julie glanced at him and back to Jo. "I'm so happy for you two."

What had they done? "Where's Lance?" The words burst out of him almost accusingly, and Julie's smile faltered.

"He, um, had to stay home. He has a lot on his schedule with work."

Something in her eyes gave him pause. "Is he coming for the wedding?"

"No, but he said to tell everyone hello."

Like he gave a shit what Lance said. Something was definitely off. She didn't seem her usual put-together self. There was an energy of sadness about her. He couldn't bear it.

"Well, I gotta run. I told Ryan I'd help him out with wedding stuff today." And now came the pain, the reality of knowing he could have made her happy, if he'd had the courage to approach her first. But he didn't and he lost his chance with her, because she'd never leave Lance.

Jo was right. Seeing Julie only made him sad.

CHAPTER 6

"Are we going to talk about your mood?" Ryan's stare focused on the teensy ribbon he was trying to work into a bow, but Pat still felt like he was under a microscope lens.

He grabbed another lace sash thing and stuffed it full of Jordan almonds. "I'm not in a mood."

It was a lie. He'd been pissy since leaving Jo's and learning that Julie was marrying that douchebag. His brain couldn't stop repeating her words.

Lance said to tell everyone hello... He made me drive home alone and doesn't appreciate me, but I love him and we're so happy...

Okay, maybe his brain went slightly off script, but her blind devotion drove him insane sometimes. And what the hell was Jo thinking, hiding Julie's engagement from him? That was crucial information that should have been brought to his immediate attention.

He shoved another handful of candy coated nuts into a dainty satchel, but this wasn't a job that could be rushed, nor was it a job for big hands. The damn candies went pinging everywhere.

"Yeah, you're just a ray of freaking sunshine," his brother commented dryly.

Pat scooped up the scattered nuts. "Sorry. I just have some stuff on my mind."

A silent minute passed where they both focused hard on tying little bows. How the hell did women make this stuff look so easy? When Maggie and Perrin showed them how to twist the ribbon and tie off the favors, he assumed him and Ryan could have the box of fancy baggies and nuts done in no time. They'd been tying bows for over an hour and their pile was pathetic.

"Is it Mum? I heard she booked an appointment with the realtor this morning. You know, you don't have to rush into anything."

He cut another piece of ribbon. "It's not that. Well, it is, but I always knew I'd be looking for a place. I want to be self-sufficient as soon as possible."

"See anything good this morning?"

Seriously, it was a good thing he hadn't opted to become a surgeon. His fingers were not meant for dexterous work. "The old bookstore. I wanted you to check it out. It would need some work."

"I haven't been in there since I was a kid. Couldn't even tell you what it looks like."

"The realtor texted me the lockbox code, so maybe—if you have a spare second—we could check it out."

Ryan knotted off another bow. His favors were looking less dejected than Pat's. "I'll make time. This is important, Pat."

He paused. "I know, but the wedding is going to be here in—"

"Nope. You don't get to push off your important stuff for

mine. I *want* to give you a hand with this. It's a big deal. I psyched you're moving back home and we can hang out whenever we want again. Whatever you need, I'm here for you."

He appreciated that, because if he bought the old bookshop, he was going to need a hand renovating. "Do people actually eat these things?"

Ryan shrugged. "I have no clue. But apparently, they're expected. I had like six women ask me if we ordered the Jordan Almonds. I never even heard of them."

Pat frowned. "Who the hell is Jordan, anyway, and why are his almonds so famous?"

They worked their way through several more bags.

"So, are we going to discuss your news?"

"What new—oh. That."

His brother frowned at him. "Quite a…uh…one-eighty from our old talks."

He didn't need him to clarify. Growing up together, Ryan had suffered through way too many diatribes of why Julie was the perfect girl for him. And as much as she and Jo were twins, they were as opposite as night and day.

"Well, you know how these things go."

His brother paused from tying bows. "What does that mean?"

Pat didn't have a clue. "Did you know she was marrying him?"

"Who?"

"Julie, she's marrying Lance."

Ryan's brows lifted. "Jeeze. Good luck to her." He studied him but Pat kept his focus on stuffing nuts into bags. "How are you taking that?"

The Jo thing was actually a decent shield, so he didn't have to admit how much the news was crushing him. He shrugged. "It is what it is. I've moved on."

"Have you?"

Suddenly irritated and—*why were these damn nuts so slippery?* He flung the delicate satchel onto the table. "Say what you want to say, Ry."

His brother sat back and folded his arms over his chest, pinning him with a knowing glare. It was that damn big brother look he did so well, the one that always made Pat feel inexperienced and uncertain beside his confidence.

"Fine. Marriage is serious. And, unless you're so into a girl that you can't bear the thought of being away from her for more than a day, I'd say it's not the right woman. And at this stage, couples typically can't keep their hands off each other. You and Jo… Well, I didn't really see a spark yesterday."

"Maybe we're just more discrete."

"Pat…"

He met his brother's stare. "What?"

What did he want him to say? Why did the truth matter? The woman he wanted was taken. She was getting married, and he'd never have a chance to show her how great they could be. He figured she'd eventually come around and they'd have their time, but life went from childhood to adulthood overnight. Now, they were all stuck in this quicksand of adulting.

"They're not married yet." Ryan didn't need to clarify that he was referring to Julie and Lance.

"Well, she's not the sort of girl to make polar shifts."

"How do you know?"

"Because I know her."

"You haven't hung out with her in years. People change."

Not Julie. She was reliable and as even-keeled as a woman could be. "We have to get these done. Maggie's gonna be home soon."

"Forget the nuts for a second and level with me."

At the sharp command in his voice, Pat grit his teeth then snapped, "What do you want me to say, Ryan? That she was my first choice? Fine. Julie was first. She'll always be before anyone else, because I loved her since kindergarten. But I fucked up and was too paralyzed by the doubts in my head to do anything about it. I didn't have the balls to ask her out, because I was too afraid of damaging our friendship and losing her. But I lost her anyway. Is that what you want to hear? Does that fix something for you? Because from where I stand, I'm fucked no matter who I end up with. And hearing how pathetic I am doesn't fix shit."

A heaviness settled over his chest like a tightening vise, squeezing until he could barely draw in a single breath. Ryan's stunned expression seemed to add to the pressure.

"I'm sorry—"

"It's cool."

"No, it's not." Without looking at him, he heard the sincere apology in his tone.

Pat blew out a breath. "You were just asking. I shouldn't have snapped. You're getting married—"

"Will you knock it off. Stop acting like a wedding is some sort of immunity ceremony. I get that life isn't going to uncomplicate itself for my big day. I can deal with some drama. You're not going to spoil anything for me."

Pat shook his head, disgusted with himself and his outburst. "I'm supposed to be helping you."

"You're helping me, just by standing by my side as my best man. I just want my brother there with me." He picked up a tied up bag of nuts and tossed it back in the pile. "None of this other shit matters."

"But Maggie said the favors have to be—"

"Maggie doesn't care. She's been through this before. She knows what really counts and that's what she needs from me.

She couldn't give two shits about bows and candy and all this other crap Mum said we should have."

If that was true, then his brother really found a good one. "You're lucky."

Ryan laughed. "No one ever called me lucky when it came to romance."

"Yeah, well, in the end, you lucked out. She seems really cool."

He and his brother never were ashamed of wanting love and a family. That was how they were raised. But neither of them had an easy time finding such things. He was glad at least one of them had lucked out.

"Look," Ryan said, his tone delicate. "If Jo's the one for you, you have my total support. But if she's not, if there's even the slightest chance you could be happier with someone else, hold out. You know I love Jo, but I love you more and I want to see you happy. I want you to feel what I feel when I look at Maggie."

Pat wanted that too. "Thanks." Lying was exhausting. "The Jo thing..." He hesitated. "Her mother..." Again, he struggled to find a simple explanation. "Sometimes something seems harmless but ends up way more complicated—"

There was a heavy knock at the front door and they both turned. A small silhouette blurred on the other end of the glass, and Ryan rose from the dining room table to see who it was.

He opened the front door and Pat listened, his eyes focused back on the bows. "Hey, Jo," Ryan greeted.

"Hey, Ry." She followed him into the house with the grace of an ox. "Pat, I need to talk to you about something—*alone.*"

Ryan lifted a brow but kept all commentary to himself. Even if he hadn't had the chance to fully explain the situation, his brother wasn't an idiot, and he was beginning to get the picture. "Better do what the missus wants."

Jo flinched and he had to laugh. It was too easy to bust her chops with the domestic labels. Pat stood, glad to have a break from stuffing almonds. "Happy wife, happy life, right?"

Jo rolled her eyes. "Just take your good old time. Not like I came over here in a rush or anything."

He frowned at the urgency in her voice and followed her outside to the front porch. "What's up?"

"They broke up."

"What?" He instinctively knew she was talking about Julie and Lance. He knew he sensed something off with her. "When? Why?"

"I don't know the whole story. She said she's still processing. It just happened, like not even forty-eight hours ago. They had a fight, and she left."

"Wait, did they *actually* break up? Or did they argue and she left angry? There's a difference."

"I don't know. She seems really unsure right now and not herself. God, I hate that he can do that to her."

His molars locked. The thought of that asshole doing anything to Julie made him see red. "What *exactly* did she say?"

"She said she needed to come home to think. I checked her car. There's a box on the front seat."

"Just the front seat?" She'd lived with Lance for years. Her life wouldn't fit in just a few boxes, let alone one.

"Well...yeah."

Something didn't feel right. It was as if he was too afraid to actually believe she might truly be done with him. "What did your mom say?"

"She doesn't know—"

"Oh, well there you go." He threw up his hands in frustration.

"What do you mean?"

"Jo, they had a fight. He's a dick. But he's always been a

dick. She's not going to move home with one box. And if she was truly *moving home,* your mother and father would know."

"I thought you'd be happy."

"I would, if they were actually over."

Her brow creased. "You weren't there, Pat. You didn't see the desperation in her eyes. Whether it's over or not, she wants to leave. I think she's depressed and scared. Maybe even a little embarrassed."

His distrust morphed into concern. Julie was once one of his closest friends, but over time he made the healthy, self-preserving decision to distance himself. It was too painful keeping her in his world while she built her life with another man.

But what if this was true, and they were actually over? She would need time, of course, but what if this was his shot? What if he finally had a chance to get the girl? Then it occurred to him…

"Damn it!"

"What?"

"She thinks we're engaged!"

True guilt flashed in Jo's eyes. "We'll break up. We can make a whole thing of it, and tell everyone we decided we're better as friends."

He paced away from her and raked his hands through his hair. "How did I ever let you convince me to go along with this?"

"Me? It was your idea! You're the one who begged me to come home with you! You suggested it!"

"I said we would lie to your mom and say we were *dating*. It was your crazy idea to tell the whole town we're engaged!"

"That was your cousin!"

"Well, if you tell one McCullough anything, you might as well broadcast it to the world!"

"Why are you yelling at me!"

"Because I'm angry!"

The front door opened and Ryan poked his head out. "Hey, guys, I know we're on the outskirts here, but I do have neighbors. Could you keep it down or at least come inside?"

"It's fine. I'm leaving anyway."

"Jo, wait—"

She shot up her middle finger and marched away. He cursed and turned toward his brother.

"Should you go after her?"

"No. Do you have something to drink?"

"Beer?"

"I'll take six."

BEING AWAY at school and then living on his own away from the insanity of his big Irish family had dulled his instincts. He should have known better. He should have expected a response to his engagement, but he'd been so preoccupied with helping Ryan pick his gift for Maggie and helping him figure out a seating chart for their overgrown family that he'd let his guard down.

Apparently, Jo hadn't expected anything either, because when they walked into O'Malley's that night to the scream of his entire family yelling congratulations, she looked just as stunned as him.

She smiled nervously and stepped to his side. Through a plastered on smile, she mumbled, "Did you know about this?"

"Nope."

Crepe paper wedding bells hung from the moldings, and a pile of silver wrapped presents were stacked on a back table. For a split-second, Pat prayed this was some sort of wedding shower for Ryan and Maggie, but when he saw his brother's expression, he knew it wasn't.

Ryan was in on the surprise, and his earlier suspicions that Pat's engagement to Jo might have the shelf life of a banana, left a teasing glint in his eye. As an older brother, he would always take pleasure in ordinary family tortures.

Pat's horrified gaze scanned the crowd and he spotted Julie and her parents. Why was she standing with them instead of the younger crowd?

Sheilagh approached and bumped his hip with hers. "Well, this escalated quickly. How the hell you gonna break it to them now?"

He and Jo scowled at her.

"Smile, you two!" They turned and his mother snapped a photo with her phone. "Oh, you look completely shocked! That's a keeper!"

They were shuffled into the back, where a spread of food had been laid out. After eating, they were forced to open presents. It was by far the most awkward experience of his life. And worst of all, many of his relatives gave him cards filled with money, expressing that it was both an engagement present *and* a graduation gift. How the hell was he ever going to return all of this?

He needed air. Sneaking out front, he swiped off his glasses and pinched the bridge of his nose, trying to think of the best way out of this clusterfuck. He should just go back inside, take Jo's hand, and say they had a confession.

"I know... Me too..."

He paused at the soft voice coming from around the corner. Following the sound, he crept a few steps forward and spotted Julie. Her back was to him as she held her phone close to her ear.

"Lance, you know why..."

Lance? His mind practically hissed. Why was she calling him? Or had he called her? He knew they weren't through.

"I love you, too."

She loved him? He rolled his eyes.

"No, don't come here. Just…keep your appointments. I know you need to work. It's fine."

They didn't sound like they were fighting. They sounded like a couple juggling busy lives and conflicting schedules. He should have never listened to Jo, should have never gotten his hopes up.

"Okay… Me, too. Bye."

He stepped into the shadows as she used the back door to go inside. He could kill Jo for giving him false hope. That's it. He was through with this lie and fed up with the Cooks altogether. Marching back inside, he went hunting for his *fiancée.*

"Hey, Pat, come sit with us—"

"Not now," he snapped at Sheilagh. "Have you seen Jo?"

"Uh, I think she's in the back."

He made a beeline past the pool tables but came up short when he stepped into what seemed a private conversation between her and her sister. Taking a step back, he hovered at the doorway out of sight.

"Don't worry about me, Jules," Jo's voice was casual, in that typical tone she adopted when hiding the truth. "I'm fine."

"I know how his family can be."

Pat frowned. *His* family? She had some nerve. Of course, his family could be a lot. And yes, they sometimes took things to the extreme, like throwing an engagement party less than twenty-four hours after a proposal was announced. And they had their fair share of shotgun weddings and actual groom shootings in their family history, but what family didn't? At least their intensions were good.

"We barely got to talk about this," Julie continued, her voice soft and full of concern. "There has to be a reason you didn't tell me he proposed—or even mention that you two were dating. I just want to make sure this is what you want. You two always seemed more like…friends."

His jaw locked. Who was she to nose around in Jo's life? Like she had any sort of credibility where relationships were concerned. She dated, lived with, and got engaged to the biggest asshole in their class. And she was *never* going to leave him.

All of his disappointment and insecurities morphed into something cold and angry. He wanted to hurt her for all the times she didn't notice him. See if, *just once*, he could get any sort of response out of her.

Crossing the threshold into the hall, he pasted on a bright smile. "There you are."

Jo tensed when he pulled her close and pressed a kiss on her temple.

"I was looking all over for you." He glanced at Julie, who watched him closely, then turned his attention back to his blushing bride as her annoyance at being manhandled morphed into mute fury. "My mum wanted to grab another picture of us. Something for the newspaper, to make the announcement."

Jo scowled at him, and he poked her nose, giving her a little bop on the tip, because he knew how much she hated corny public displays of affection from cheesy couples.

"I know you hate pictures, honey. But you look beautiful. Doesn't she, Jules?"

Julie smiled. "Always. I wish I got your bone structure and coloring." She studied them a moment longer. "I see it now. I don't know why I couldn't see it before. You two are perfect together—best friends, the way it's supposed to be."

"Yup." He met Julie's stare hoping to find a spark of disappointment but only saw acceptance. "She's the one for me."

He once swore he'd never hurt her. As a matter of fact, there had been several times he suffered in discomfort, just to make her more comfortable. But she never saw him as anything more than a friend. And seeing her plain indifference now, crushed him.

Something dark and damaged inside of him wanted to punish her for that shortcoming. Turning his stare to Jo, he smiled. "My perfect Jo." Then he did something he never imagined doing and dropped his lips to hers.

Jo's eyes widened, but it was too late. Before she could object, he was kissing her. It was the most unchoreographed, wrong sort of kiss he'd ever experienced in his life. He imagined kissing Jo would be the closest he could come to kissing a sister, if he had one. But he kept his stomach in check and forced himself through it.

When he pulled away, he glanced at Julie. She gave him a strange smile and walked away, mumbling something about giving them a few minutes alone. When he turned back to Jo, she slapped him. Hard.

"What the psycho ass fuck was that?" She cleaned off her lips on the back of her hand. "Do you always use that much tongue? Jesus, I feel violated."

His face stung and he scowled at her, too angry to make any excuses. "They're not broken up. The next time you want to gossip, get your facts straight." With that, he stomped away.

CHAPTER 7

Jo caught up to him before he could fall too far into his own self-destructing spiral. She yanked him to a stop and shoved him into the men's bathroom, apparently undisturbed by Mac, a local lumberjack, taking a leak in the urinal four feet away.

"That's it!" she snapped. "For years—*years*—I've watched you come up with every excuse under the sun *not* to tell Julie how you feel. And now that she's finally single, you're out of excuses. You're scared if you tell her your feelings—you know, verbalize them—she might shoot you down. And this time, you can't blame the other guy for getting there first. But let's get one thing clear. You *do not,* I repeat, you absolutely *do not* get to blame me. They *are* broken up, Patrick. I don't know what you heard, but I got my information directly from the source. If you want her, tell her. Stop looking for reasons to wait when you've already waited so long."

The urinal flushed, and Mac awkwardly stepped past them and scooted out the door.

"I heard her on the phone with him."

"So? And are we going to completely ignore the fact that Mac didn't wash his hands?"

"So, they didn't sound broken up!"

"I take that as a yes on the Mac thing."

"Forget about Mac! What the hell is going on? *If* they're broken up, why would she talk to him like that?"

"Did you ever think it might be easier for her? You get exhausted just discussing the weather with Lance. Put yourself in her shoes for a second. She left him, Pat. She's doing her best to stay gone. In one hour, I witnessed him call her phone thirty times. She's probably going to have to change her number. This isn't easy for her. And I know he's threatening to come here. She doesn't want a scene. And what the hell was that kiss? You're full throttle self-sabotaging!"

He took a step back, shrinking by the second after such a small-minded display of jealousy and anger. Kissing Jo only added more fuel to this flaming dumpster fire of a charade.

"We have to fix this. We're lying to the whole town and our families." They were lying to *Julie*.

"You're right. I never meant for one little fib to get so blown out of proportion."

"We'll give back all the cards."

"Who buys engagement presents that early anyway?"

"I know, right?"

"I liked that espresso machine."

He rolled his eyes. "It's over."

They both eyed the door and hesitated, neither of them eager to go announce to their families that they lied.

"My mom's going to try to fix me up with Tobin."

He glanced at her. "You could just tell her."

"I could, but I'd suffer so much bullshit after the fact. It's just not worth it. I am what I am."

"Maybe she'll surprise you."

"She won't. I know my mother. At least this way, the *fake* me still gets to come home for holidays."

The sad truth was, the real Jo wouldn't be welcome. She never was. And that was why Jo kept her reality hundreds of miles away from her family.

He took her hand and gave it a comforting squeeze. Then it hit him. He was losing her. Moving home meant letting her go, because she'd never come back here for more than a day or two.

She smiled sadly, as if reading his mind. "I'll be okay. I have Jeff and Shay and Dina to keep me company. And you'll be back to visit."

He nodded, knowing time would slowly stretch those visits farther and farther apart until they eventually lost any sense of pattern.

"Come on. Let's go find Jules," she said.

He reached for the door but came up short when she grabbed his sleeve.

"Pat, wait."

He paused and stared down at her. "What is it?"

True uncertainty flashed in her eyes. "Even if they're over, she's fragile. You should tell her, but…be patient. Don't rush things. Show her you're not a meaningless rebound. Show her you can wait as long as it takes and that you're serious."

He'd waited his entire life. "We'll see how it goes." He held the door and followed her out, only to stagger to a stop.

Julie was waiting with her purse and keys in hand, looking for them in the back hall. "There you two are. I'm going to head home. I have a headache."

He glanced at Jo, needing her courage. "We have to tell you something, Jules."

"What's the matter?" concern contorted her face, and he noted the lines of stress around her eyes. She looked incredibly tired, blood from a stone tired, tired beyond anything a night or week of sleep could fix.

Jo removed the ring from her left hand and held it up. "We found this ring walking home from a bar in the city one night. Pat didn't give it to me."

Julie frowned. "Well, it looks real."

She wasn't getting it. His chest hurt at the inevitable betrayal he had to deliver. "We're not engaged."

Her frown deepened. "What?"

"It was a lie to get mom off my back," Jo explained.

Julie's head cocked, as if she'd been so convinced they were a couple that this somehow broke a piece of her thinking. "But...everyone's here...celebrating your engagement."

Jo bit her lip. "Things got really out of hand really quickly."

"You lied." Her frown shifted to a scowl as she looked at her sister. "Both of you." When her stare cut into him, it burned like a hot ember burrowing into his soul.

He couldn't bare the look of betrayal in her eyes. "We never meant to hurt anyone."

"But you lied. You lied to *me*."

"We're sorry," Jo apologized.

Julie shook her head and took a step back. "I... I have to go." She turned and rather than exiting the front of the bar, made a quick escape out the back.

He cursed. "I'm going after her—"

"She needs to process—"

"I'm going after her, Jo. Tell everyone I said goodnight." He bolted out the back and jogged into the dark lot. "Julie?"

The sound of metal keys falling to the pavement alerted him to where she was. She bent to pick up her keys, obviously shaken and upset, as the headlights to her Benz flashed bright in the dark night.

"Go away, Patrick."

He was by her side, closing his hand over the keys and preventing her escape. "Don't leave."

Something seemed to rupture behind her eyes as she looked at him, a world of turmoil and distress staring back at him. "You lied to me. *You.* I never thought..." Her words broke off as she choked on a sob.

He pulled her into his arms, trying to comfort her but she stiffened. His hand rubbed down her back, attempting to soothe her. "It was a stupid thing, and I never meant for it to go this far. Please believe me when I say I never meant to lie to you. I'm still the boy that was your best friend, and I'd rather cut off my own hand than hurt you. No matter how much we've changed, that has stayed the same."

The tension in her shoulders slowly relaxed. "I don't understand."

"Jo didn't feel like dealing with blind dates and everything spiraled. It was stupid. There's nothing to understand."

She pulled back a few inches and looked up at him, her pale lashes wet with tears and her eyes confused. She was so delicate yet so fierce, so obviously suffering some sort of personal crisis that appeared a struggle to bear.

He tucked a strand of hair behind her ear and whispered, "What did Lance do to you?"

Her chin trembled and her gaze shifted away. "I did it to myself."

He frowned. Something had happened to her. This wasn't the same Julie he'd known through grade school or the strong-willed girl he watched become a woman in high school.

He thought back to the numerous psychology classes he took and all the studies he'd read on trauma. "Are you leaving him?"

Her lashes lowered. "Break ups are complicated after being with the same person for years. We're at the end, but it feels far from over. I think our relationship's been dying for years."

Did she blame herself for not leaving sooner? "Sometimes, people make a habit of feeling guilty for their survival instincts. We can't shut them off. And when survival doesn't include an immediate escape from a bad situation, it can be mistaken for acceptance. But it's all part of finding a way out. Even the early, smallest steps matter in the longest journeys."

He hoped he didn't sound trite or condescending. His chest burned with uncertainty. All he wanted was to comfort her.

Her breath hitched with a jagged sob, and she hugged him tight, startling him. He slowly closed his arms around her, protectively guarding her from whatever demons she feared and pressed his lips to the top of her head.

"It's okay. It's okay."

Soft whimpers heated his chest through the damp cotton of his shirt as he held her while she cried. The front door of the bar opened, and they both stiffened. She looked up at him, her panicked eyes pleading for him to get her away from there.

"I don't want to see anyone."

He'd risk his own life to rescue her. His protective instincts shot into motion. "Come with me." He walked her to the passenger side of her car and took the keys. "I'll drive."

After a quick adjustment to the driver's seat, he backed out of the lot and steered the car down Main Street. He hadn't thought about where they could go, they were both sort of homeless and squatting at their parents' for the time being, but he knew he needed to take her away, someplace quiet, where she could think and possibly talk.

He remembered the bookstore and headed that way, pulling up the lockbox code in the text message the realtor had sent him. It was after ten, so most of the Main Street stores were closed, and there was plenty of parking. As he slid into a space across from the old bookstore, she looked up and frowned.

"What are we doing here?"

"I want to show you something." He shut off the car and came around to open her door. She hesitated, but he was patient.

He held out his hand, and she slowly took it, rising from the car and following him to the bolted door. She watched silently as he entered the code and removed the key from the lockbox. When the door gave way, he felt a sense of relief.

She paused on the outside of the threshold, and he looked back, his silence telling her he could be as patient as she needed.

"Are we breaking in?"

"No. I have the code and permission from the realtor."

She looked up at the dark rafters and took a step inside. Dusty, hollow bookshelves entombed the front half of the store, but the back half was mostly empty.

He flipped a switch, but the electric must have been shut off. "Just give me a second."

Searching the drawers of what used to be the old cashier desk, he found a jar candle and a pack of matches. In the back, he located an old shawl hanging on a peg and a few empty cardboard boxes.

His phone vibrated, creating a glow in the shadows as his brother's name flashed on the screen. Glancing at Julie who stood by the front window staring at the dark street, he kept his voice quiet and answered the call. "Hey."

The racket from the bar was brash and contrasted with the silence of his surroundings. "Where are you?"

"Something came up. I had to leave."

A moment passed where only the background noise of his loud family came from the phone. "Julie?" Ryan finally asked.

"Yeah."

"I figured, when I couldn't find either of you."

"Do me a favor and cover for me."

"Okay. Does Jo know—"

"She knows."

Another pause. "This is messy, Pat."

"This is life."

"All right. Call me if you need something."

"Thanks, Ry."

CHAPTER 8

Pat ended the call and tore open an empty cardboard box, breaking the sides apart. Returning to the main area of the store, he laid the cardboard flat on the floor while Julie watched curiously. He lit the candle and placed it on a stack of books to the side. Shaking out the shawl, he held it out for her, as if it were a cape suited for royalty.

The most fragile smile curled her mouth as she stepped into it. They sat on the flattened box and leaned against the wall, staring at the flickering candlelight.

"Why did you bring me here?"

"It's the only place I could think of where we could be alone."

Her head turned and she looked at him. "You wanted to get me alone?"

"I wanted a place where we could talk—or sit. I just wanted to be with you."

A pucker formed between her brows. "You and Jo—"

"Are only friends. I swear. We've never been anything more."

"But you kissed her—"

"Another stupid move on my part. As soon as you left, she hit me for it."

That got a small smile out of her.

"She's my best friend, Jules, but that's it. I wanted her to come home with me, but she didn't want to get fixed up with anyone by your mom and her friends, so I told her I'd pretend to be her boyfriend. It was stupid."

Her smile stretched to her eyes. "Not stupid. Sweet. You love her."

"As much as a guy can love his best friend, yeah, I do. There isn't much I wouldn't do for your sister."

Something sad flashed in her eyes. "Why did you stop talking to me? It used to be the three of us, you, me, and Jo. What happened?"

"Well, you started dating Lance. Then I went away to school, and I guess, we just lost touch."

"I was so mad at you."

"Me?" Her words shocked him.

"Yeah. You just cut me off. And then you took Jo away."

He blinked, trying to see it from her perspective. He supposed it might seem like that, but that had never been his intention. "I never meant to hurt you. And I didn't *take* Jo away. *She* ran away."

"I know. But sometimes it was easier to blame you. I resented you for a long time, wondering why my sister loved you more than me, why she couldn't stay here with me. After she left, Jasper Falls was never the same."

He hadn't considered what it would have been like for her without her twin sister. They had always been inseparable.

"It wasn't about you. Not for Jo. She needed to get out of here. This place… It's not good for her."

"I don't believe that. I know she and my parents argue, but if she just—"

"No." He had to side with Jo on this one. "They don't accept her for who she is. In the city, she's free. She can be whoever she wants to be. She's beautiful there. Happy."

"You two were never dating?"

"I told you, we're just friends."

"It's not just you, is it? I mean, there have been other guys who seemed right for her. She doesn't..."

It wasn't his place to have this discussion. "You need to talk to your sister. I think it would clear up a lot of stuff for you."

Her head tipped back, leaning against the wall, and her eyes closed. "Do you know what it's like to try to keep your eyes as wide open as humanly possible and still feel like the blindest person in any room?"

"You're not blind. Some people are just really good at hiding their secrets." She remained still and silent, keeping her eyes closed, like she hadn't heard his words. His voice softened. "Jules, what did he do to you?"

A lone tear slid from her lashes and disappeared beneath her jawline. Her lips formed a thin line. "I don't know. I don't know anything for certain anymore."

"You can talk to me. I'm your friend."

Her eyes remained closed. He assumed she wouldn't answer, but there seemed some sort of internal struggle happening beneath the surface, as if she wanted to explain but physically couldn't. So, help him, God, if that man laid a hand on her...

"Did he hit you?"

She shook her head. "Sometimes I wished he would. At least then, I'd know I wasn't imagining things. I'd know I wasn't crazy."

"Was he verbally abusive to you?"

Her lips trembled as her frown deepened. "Not always. But when he was, he did it so precisely, it could happen in front of a room full of people and no one would realize it was happening, including me."

He always hated Lance, and he wasn't sure he could handle disliking him any more than he already did, but sure enough, it was happening. "Can you give me an example?"

She sniffled and exhaled softly, her eyes still resting closed as the tension slipped from her face. "He was charming. Every woman I knew envied the way he treated me. He was the guy who held doors, pulled out chairs, and showed up with a long stem rose for no reason at all."

Maybe he didn't want to hear this after all.

"Lance loved being the center of attention. It never bothered me, because I always felt privileged to simply hang in his orbit. I mean, who am I? I'm no one."

He wanted to shake her. She was *not* no one. *She* was the showstopper, the person people actually came to see. Lance was a piece of shit everyone tolerated simply to be near her.

"There's an old saying," she continued. "*Some people cut the heads off others to make themselves feel taller.* I didn't realize Lance was cutting off my head, because he did it so subtly over such a long period of time, but eventually, I woke up and couldn't think for myself anymore. It was as if he'd performed a lobotomy by scraping away thin layers, just paper thin slivers, year after year. I truly feel like he stole a part of my thinking and it scares me, because I can't find it. If that doesn't sound crazy I don't know what does."

She looked the same, still indefinably beautiful, but also looked weak, like she'd been the victim of something awful. "How would he do it?"

"First, it wasn't directed at me. I'd catch him in little exaggerations. If his car cost seventy thousand, he'd tell people it was worth a hundred. I never corrected him, because it would have embarrassed both of us. Then those exaggerations shifted into bigger lies, like when his co-worker got a promotion, he told our friends *he* got one."

"Did you ever question him about it?" He knew Lance liked to brag, it was the biggest reason why people avoided him.

"A few times, but he had a way of twisting things around. And when I questioned him, he somehow turned the focus on my flaws, saying I was flighty or accusing me of misremembering things. He'd lie so often and so convincingly about the littlest things, I'd get lost in the minutia and be unable to trace my way back to the truth." She shrugged. "Maybe I *was* remembering things wrong. The more he repeated a lie, the more I figured it must be true. It was as if he so genuinely believed himself, I was the one misunderstanding. I'm not as confident as him."

But she had been at one time. "He was gaslighting you, Julie."

She finally opened her eyes but didn't look at him. Her focus remained on the shadows across the room, like she were staring into another time and place. "I think that's what it was. I've read a few books, and he fits all the criteria, the lies, the repetition, and the escalation. Once, I really challenged him, and he doubled down on the lie so many times, screaming at me with such fury, I figured I had to be wrong. Nothing could make me that angry with him. I figured…such conviction could only come from a loyalty to the truth."

"But you knew he was lying."

She paused and looked at him then. "No, Pat. I didn't know anything anymore. I just knew I didn't want to fight and I was sorry I brought it up. After a while, we lived in an alternate reality, where he got to rewrite the facts any way it suited him."

"Didn't others see what he was doing?"

"If they did, they ignored it. I know you never cared for

Lance, but he's really quite popular in Maryland. We have a lot of friends, and he's very charismatic. People love his energy and want to be close to him. It's like a drug. His one friend, Tim, would agree with anything he said. It's pathetic. One time..."

"One time?"

Her brow creased and she looked down at her wringing hands. "One time I came home from the store, and Tim and Lance were watching the game. I came in and asked him to help me unload the bags from the car. I even made a comment that it was halftime and there wasn't much to carry. Lance said sure but never moved. Tim stared at me the whole time—he did that a lot. I always felt like he was watching me. A few trips back-and-forth from the garage and I finally emptied the car. I said something to Lance about leaving me to do it all by myself. He looked at me and said I never asked for help."

The exasperation in her face made it clear she had. Fanning out her hands, she turned to Pat and said, "I had a whole conversation with him about giving me a hand. He even asked if I bought more chips and I said yes. His friend witnessed the whole thing. But as he sat there and told me I never said a word, Tim agreed with him. I spent the rest of the day laying down, wondering if I had some sort of episode."

Because that was what gaslighters did, they wore down their victims. "How long were things like this going on?"

"Part of me thinks he was always doing it, but it only became evident when I moved in with him, particularly after I stopped working."

"Because you were more reliant on him?"

"Yes. It was like he knew he could push my buttons and I had no leverage to push back. He kept me so tied up in emotional knots, I didn't feel confident about finding another job. And I didn't want to come home. I really, with all my heart, wanted to make us work. I tried everything to make him happy, but I was *always* screwing up."

"It's not screwing up when someone consistently changes the rules without warning."

She nodded, but her eyes remained sad. "I started keeping lists of things I did, so I wouldn't second guess myself. The amount of time I dedicated to creating a paper trail was ridiculous. Some days I'd get so furious with myself, because I knew this wasn't normal, healthy relationship behavior. I'd think about leaving, but he always sensed when I was at wits' end and he would do something incredibly sweet. I'm not talking about small gestures. I'm talking about redefining big gestures, like taking a week off to take me away. We'd spend days laughing and making love, and I'd leave *convinced* everything was better, sure that I'd made things worse in my head than they actually were. Lance used to tell me I exaggerated situations in my head, because I had too much time on my hands."

"Projecting. He was accusing you of his own behaviors."

"I guess."

They sat in silence for several minutes. He needed a moment to process everything she said, certain it was abuse but also certain such an obscure form of slow manipulation could feel like insanity gradually setting in. But she wasn't crazy.

"Have you talked to anyone about this, Julie?"

"No. I've read a few books and that's helping, but there was no way I could have met with a psychologist without Lance knowing. And if he knew, he would have said I was being dramatic or overly sensitive."

Because God forbid she actually get help and figure a way out from under his control. "How did you get away?"

"We had a fight about the wedding. He said he was going

then acted like I totally imagined it. It was a bad fight. I told him I was done and he snapped." She was quiet for a moment, likely replaying some of the harsh things he said. "The next morning, I got up, threw a few things in a box, packed a bag, and I left. He thinks I'm coming back."

A chill seemed to shudder across his heart. "Are you?"

"I don't want to."

"Then don't." He turned to better face her and took her hand. "Don't go back to that, Jules. Don't go back to him."

Her gaze darted away as her eyes flooded with tears. "I'm trying. I hate who I am with him, but it's like he's inside of me, this insidious voice I can't outrun. He won't leave me alone long enough to think things through—"

"Because he knows time will make you stronger."

"I don't feel strong. I feel confused and broken and scared."

He didn't have a right to touch her, but he wanted desperately to comfort her. "Listen to me. You are not a weak woman. You're smart and beautiful and resilient. He's the weak one. That's why he is the way he is. Every time he acts big, it's because he feels threatened and small. You don't need him, Julie. *He* needs you."

"He doesn't need me. He's already said he'd move on if I left."

"So? Let him. He'd be doing you a favor."

Her gaze filled with sorrow as she stared up at him with bleak, hollow hope, as fragile as glass, in her shimmering eyes. "He's all I've ever known. I've never been with anyone else. What if he's right? What if there's something wrong with me—"

"No," he snapped. "There is absolutely *nothing* wrong with *you,* so get that thought out of your head right now."

"Then why is he the only man who's ever wanted me?"

His jaw practically unhinged. Was she kidding? "Julie,

guys have wanted you since first grade. What the hell are you talking about?" He still remembered punching Steve Gumbo in the stomach when he said he was gonna marry her. They were only in middle school then, but Pat already decided she was his.

"Who? That's ridiculous."

Now he did look at her like she was crazy. "No, it's not. Trust *me*."

Her expression shuttered. "I can't trust anyone until I can trust myself. And you lied to me."

His gaze lowered in shame. "I'm sorry. I know that doesn't change what I did, but I can make you a promise." He met her stare and looked directly into her eyes. "I swear, I'll never lie to you again. From here on, you'll have nothing but absolute honesty from me."

Her smile was slow and delicate. "Tell me who wanted me. I don't believe there were all these guys like you say."

He sat back and shook off his shock. "Wow, you played me."

"No, I'm mad about the lie. But if you swear to tell me the truth, let's test your word."

He had to laugh. It was the first glimpse of her usual, clever, feisty self, and he'd take that any day over the weepy, uncertain creature who cried in his arms. Was this it? Was this when it would finally come out?

He hesitated a moment, considering if this was a bad decision or the perfect opportunity to finally tell her the truth, the one secret he'd always wanted her to know.

"You have to promise me something first."

"Okay."

"Promise you'll stay with me until the candle burns out."

Her smile was almost childlike. "Okay."

He drew in a galvanizing breath and let it out slowly. "Jeff Fields had a crush on you in fifth grade."

"Ew, he used to pull my hair."

"Exactly. In sixth grade, it was John Fox. In seventh—that was a big year for you—"

"Boobs."

"Exactly. In seventh, it was Kelly McCullough, Rich Stack, Jim Brice, and Ron Johnson."

"Kelly McCullough had a crush on *me*?" she sounded almost thrilled.

"Yes." His cousin was easily the best looking guy in Jasper Falls and could have gotten any girl he wanted, regardless of their age, even back then. The only reason he didn't go after Julie, was because Pat begged him not to.

"Wow." She smiled. "I never knew I was that popular."

Remembering how many guys he had run interference with, exhausted him. "Then in eighth grade it was Lance Bassett."

Her smile vanished. "Lance always had a gift for getting exactly what he wanted."

"But he wasn't the one who wanted you most."

She met his stare, her eyes questioning. His heart raced in a riotous pattern, beating hard then faster until it felt ready to burst out of his chest.

"Who wanted me most?" she rasped.

He held her stare, willing her to read the thoughts right from his head. He could see it all, playing like a carousel of memories through his mind. The day she shared her pudding cup in kindergarten, the time he scraped his knee after falling off his bike and she helped him walk it home, the time she threw up in the lake when she watched him hook a worm, the day they rescued a bird that had fallen from its nest, the time he pecked her cheek just before he blew out the candles on his birthday cake—wishing with all of his birthday magic that she might love him half as much as he loved her. It was all there, an abundance of nostalgia he could hear, see, and smell, as real as the clothes on his skin and the air in his lungs. She was everything he'd always wanted, and the one thing he accepted he'd never have.

"Pat?" His name was an almost silent plea in the shadows as she searched his stare.

"I've loved you since the day I met you, Jules."

He saw it then, the innocent truth that she never knew. "But…you never said anything."

"I was always waiting for the right time. Then…I waited too long."

Her brow pinched and she turned her gaze to the floor. "How long?"

"Always. Since kindergarten." He softly caught her chin and turned her stare back to him. "It doesn't have to change anything, Jules. I don't expect—"

She covered his mouth and he stared over the top of her hand. "You liked me?"

He nodded, strangely loving the feel of her delicate fingers over his lips.

"Since kindergarten?"

Another nod.

She frowned. "When… When did your crush go away?"

He stared at her. Life could have been so much easier had his feelings ever waned, but every time he saw her, she was more beautiful than the last, more kind, and something inside of him demanded she was the only one for him. He lowered his gaze, and her hand fell away.

"Why didn't you tell me?"

His words, like so many other times, stuck in his throat. Thousands of confessions floated through his head. He could flatter her for days, possibly years, if his voice just once wouldn't betray him. He swallowed around the secrets clogging his throat and rasped, "It's difficult…"

Her gaze searched his. "Do you still have feelings for me?"

He was terrified by how much this woman could make him feel. "You're not easy to forget."

She seemed startled by his confession, almost in awe that he could feel such a way. Surely she had to realize how special she was. Even if she only knew half her value, she had ordinary women beat by miles.

Her face tipped, her gaze falling to her lap as a delicate blush crested her cheeks. Was that a smile? He gently tipped up her chin. "I wanted to tell you."

"Tell me now," she whispered.

He fought back a shiver. "I think about you…" Every day. "Nothing compares." There weren't words to accurately sum up the depth and breadth of his feelings. "I'd do anything for your happiness—"

His words cut off as her lips sealed to his and something buoyant and painful exploded in his chest. She pulled back, blinking up at him, waiting for him to say something, but he was speechless.

"You should have told me," she whispered, but any sign of hope was quickly doused by the sight of regret in her eyes. "It could have changed everything."

"It still can." He didn't want to think like that. He didn't want to live in the possibilities of the past. This was monumental. She finally knew. Now, they could talk about it and… His mind was going a mile a minute. "You kissed me."

Soft pink shaded her cheeks. "Sorry."

"Don't apologize." It had been an innocent kiss, just a peck really, but at the same time, it was the most important kiss of his life. "Do it again."

She laughed, the sound bashful and unsure. "Really?"

He nodded. Words were literally beyond his IQ at the moment.

Slowly, she closed the distance. Her eyes followed his, searching for reassurance. Her mouth curled with the threat of a nervous laugh. Then the warm press of her lips met his and their eyes closed as a thousand shock waves fizzed and danced between them.

His hand lifted, sliding beneath the curtain of her hair and tracing the delicate line of her jaw to pull her closer as he tilted his head. Her mouth was warm and sweet. He coaxed her lips apart with gentle dips of his tongue, which she shyly welcomed with her own. Then it happened, that moment when two people figure out the perfect rhythm and their body language begins to sing.

She rose onto her knees and pressed deeper into the kiss. His hands explored her arms and shoulders, wanting to touch as much of her as humanly possible. Her kisses tasted amazing, and he was finding it difficult not to lose himself in the sweet sensuality of it all.

"Patrick…"

His name was a potion she whispered, a spell she cast. "Julie…"

"We're kissing." She giggled against his lips, the sound full of playful awe.

"I know. I don't ever want to wake up from this dream."

"You're not dreaming."

"Sure I am." He trailed his lips down her throat, breathing in and tasting the sensitive skin over her rapidly thrumming pulse. "I've had this dream a million times before. I always wake up." He nibbled her ear, and she pinched him. "Ow!"

"See, not dreaming."

He drew back and looked into her eyes. She smiled, lips swollen and cheeks flushed. "Are we really doing this?"

She bit her lower lip, her shy glance momentarily skating away. "I was enjoying it."

Fear held him back. "Are you really through with him?" He hated dousing the light in her eyes, but he needed to know. He wasn't a fan of affairs, but more so, he couldn't have her, only to lose her in the end. He wasn't that strong of a man. "Can you truly say it's over?"

"Can you give me a reason to stay?"

Not what he wanted to hear. He could give her a million reasons, but he needed her to make this decision on her own.

"If you're truly finished with him, Julie, I'll spend every day convincing you this is where you belong. But you need to make the choice on your own. It's not about me. It's about you and what you want."

"Right now, all I want is for you to keep kissing me."

Damn her for trying to break him. "Don't do this to me if you're going to go back to him."

"Pat..."

He saw the plea in her eyes, the silent request that he not complicate things more than they already were, but he had to also protect himself. "I can't do casual with you, Jules."

Comprehension flashed in her eyes followed by something that looked like disappointment. He couldn't be her rebound, and she couldn't make any big decisions right now.

"I'm... Not in a place where I trust my decision-making. I can't promise you anything, but I know I don't want to hurt you, so maybe we should stop."

It was as honest an answer as anyone could possibly give, but it crushed him. He wanted to give her a reason to want more, a reason to pick him over any other option. He had to do something that proved he was the better man for her.

When would he ever have a chance like this again? Maybe never. It might have been another self-sabotaging act on his behalf, but he was sick of holding back his life for fear of the consequences and even more terrified that things might go back to normal and he'd lose her all over again.

Capturing her mouth with his, he kissed her with purpose, showing her all of his passion and desire, leaving them drunk with wanting. It was senseless. It was slightly desperate. It was definitely stupid, but he was sick of being cautious.

When he pulled away, they were both panting, a look of stunned surprise mirroring in their stares. His clothes itched to come off, and her nipples formed delicate peaks in the candlelight, where they pressed against her dress.

"Should we stop?" he asked, body hard with desire.

"Only if you want to."

"I don't want to."

"Then don't."

Acting on instinct, he swept a finger under the strap of her dress and trailed it down her arm. The shawl dropped to the floor and her chest lifted with labored breaths as she glanced down at what he'd done. She looked at the other strap still tight on her shoulder and back to him. He knocked it down, until only the stiffness of the material held the top of her linen dress in place.

The sweetest smile curled over her kiss-swollen lips, and his gaze followed the narrow contour of her throat. Everything about her was so delicate, like a line of perfect poetry he wanted to hold in his mouth forever.

Her palms turned upward in some sort of silent offering, as if she were surrendering to him. His throat went dry. He should walk away. He knew better. She had things to work out, and he had to keep his guard up until she made up her mind. But he lifted his hands and gently pulled down the front of her dress.

Pale, peach nipples peaked in the candlelight, soft and supple, delicate and inviting. "Jesus, you're beautiful."

"I don't think anyone's ever looked at me the way you're looking at me now."

He could stare at her for a hundred eternities. He wanted to taste every inch of her. Possess her soul. Wrap himself in her body. Bathe in her moans and make her body quiver with pleasure.

His finger brushed over her knee peeking from the hemline of her simple dress. Her skin was warm and inviting, so he trailed the touch higher, his hand disappearing under the material. Her hair partially hid her face as her head tipped down and she watched him. Heat beckoned as he passed the supple inside of her thigh, and she opening herself to him.

She looked at him, and he paused. Her head slightly nodded, and he traced the seam of her panties, finding the satin material damp and hot. He tucked a finger under the material and found her slick with arousal.

She released the most delicate moan, and her head fell back, displaying the long column of her neck. At that, the last of his restraint disappeared. His mouth was on her throat, licking and kissing as his fingers sought her heat, softly dipping and spreading her warm honey. Indulgent moans broke the silence as his kisses trailed lower, capturing the stiff tip of her breast and pulling hungrily.

Her fingers raked through his hair, holding him close and driving his need up several painful degrees, until he could take no more. He shoved her dress above her hips and plunged his fingers deep inside her, melting in warm honey of her arousal, drinking in her needy pleas, and wanting to give her more satisfaction than any man who had ever tried before.

Each touch was a privilege, every whimpered plea a directive he must follow. He always wished she was his, but the truth was, she owned him. He belonged to her, would worship and serve her any way she let him. *She* was his addiction, his deepest secret, and his darkest desire.

Her moans shattered into cries of pleasure as her body trembled beneath him, delicate shivers rippling over her flesh as her pliant limbs quivered. His name passed her lips with breathless surprise, as if she were stunned by the things he could make her feel. He coaxed out every drop of pleasure until the tension in her body melted away, and he held her in his arms.

She slowly looked up at him, her eyes heavy with lust and curiosity, her lashes full and so perfectly feminine. He cradled her bare shoulders, and her breast caught the moonlight piercing the dark. She was a goddess.

When she shivered, he pulled the discarded shawl over her arms and lifted her fully onto his lap. She said nothing, but the weight of her cheek resting against his chest, said it all. She felt safe with him.

He pressed a kiss to the top of her head, silently vowing to take care of her. His body ached with selfish desire, but she was his first priority. He seemed to have a primal need to make her feel safe and get her to trust him again.

They would take things as slow as she needed. As long as she questioned her own judgement, his words would carry little weight. But he could show her he was different. He'd show her there were good guys in this world. Men who valued women, respected them, and would never actively do anything to hurt others. He would be the *best* man she could find.

CHAPTER 9

Julie shifted, her back burning hot and her front freezing cold. But the stiff, smooth surface she slept on was not her bed. Her eyes opened as memories from the night before flooded her mind.

They were in the bookstore. She must have fallen asleep. Peeking over her shoulder, she found Pat sleeping soundly at her back. His arm looped possessively over her waist and dust motes danced in a beam of light seeping past the bookcases from the front windows.

Carefully lifting his arm, she momentarily wondered when he became so muscular. She scooted a few inches away and quickly righted her dress, unsure what to do.

Her mind continued to replay the things he'd done to her the night before and her cheeks heated. This was Patrick Clooney. Her sweet childhood best friend. She couldn't quite equate him with the man sleeping beside her, yet they were one in the same.

She meant what she told him, that she didn't trust her own decision-making right now. But last night had felt right. Being with Pat came so naturally, she wondered how she had never viewed him as more than a friend before. Yet there had been something foreign in the experience, something strangely pleasant she wasn't used to. The things he did to her, the way he made her feel… She blushed at the thought. Lance was never that attentive.

She chewed her lip. The thought of facing reality after her breakdown last night overwhelmed her. Before she realized what she was doing, she stood, found her keys, and rushed to the front door, only to draw back at the last second, when she spotted people out front.

She ducked behind a bookcase and spied through the soaped windows. What were they doing just standing there? Then she heard the lock jiggle, and she gasped.

"Shit." She ran back to where Pat slept on the floor. "Get up!" she hissed.

He groggily roused, then bolted upright—his red waves flipped against his usual cowlick and his expression confused then he smiled. "Hey."

"People are out front. They're trying to get in here."

He rubbed the sleep from his eyes, moving too slow for the crisis about to unfold. "Good morning. Did you sleep okay?"

"Pat, focus! People are literally trying to open the front door, and I'm pretty sure we weren't supposed to sleep here. Is there a back door?"

They didn't have time for pleasantries. The whole town thought he was engaged to her sister. And she hadn't told anyone, aside from Jo and Pat, about her and Lance. They had to get out of there.

The sound of the front door pressing open bolted him into action. He was on his feet and rushing her toward the back as a woman's voice approached from the other side of the tall shelves.

"Luckily, we always keep a separate key at the office.

You're actually the second person I've shown the property to this week."

Pat raced into the back, holding her hand in an unbreakable grip. A steal bar exit door hid behind stacks of boxes and he cursed, shoving them so fast they fell with a loud clatter.

"Hello?" the woman, who she assumed was the realtor, called. "Is someone back there?"

Pat slammed down the bar, and the door opened, blinding her with morning sunlight. He jumped the boxes first, then turned back to lift her over the mess of cardboard and books. Her heart spiked in her chest at the sense of being rescued. They ran down the back lot and dashed into the first alley they found.

She laughed, and he put a finger to his mouth, telling her to be quiet. When it appeared no one was following them, he let out a breath.

"So, I guess you weren't really allowed in there."

His stare shifted into something challenging and he kissed her, pressing her shoulders into the cool brick wall and sending a sharp thrill up her spine. It seemed like too much passion for this early in the day, but the fact that they were hiding in an alley and still in their clothes from last night didn't seem to bother Pat, so she didn't let it bother her.

Looping her arms around his neck, she hooked a leg over his hip and he lifted her, his hands sprawled her ribs as he devoured her with kisses. At this angle, she could feel the hard press of his arousal grinding into her. It amazed her that she could have such an effect on him.

She forgot how fun kissing could be. Maybe it was Pat, or maybe it was being back home, but she suddenly felt like a teenager again. Reckless and untethered.

"Take me somewhere, Pat. I don't want to go back to reality yet."

He pressed his forehead against hers and stared into her eyes. "I'll take you anywhere you want to go."

"I want to go somewhere no one will find us, somewhere it's just you and me."

He thought for a moment and then asked for her keys. They slipped out of the alleyway with matching expressions of two guilty kids who had been up to no good. Luckily, no one seemed to notice them.

When they got in the car, he drove them to the end of town and turned toward the mountains. Just before the highway, there was a highway.

"I'm going to make a quick stop. Do you need anything?"

"Um, a toothbrush and some food."

He parked. "I'll be right out."

~

THE MOMENT PAT made it into the pharmacy, he grabbed a basket and started filling it with anything he thought Julie might want or need. At the back of the store, he fished out his phone and called Ryan, pinning the device between his cheek and shoulder while he continued to shop.

"How's it going?" his brother answered.

"Unpredictably. Do you happen to know where Jo is?"

"Your bride-to-be?" His brother chuckled. "I think she crashed at Sheilagh's."

Thank God. He didn't want more people finding out the truth until they were all present and able to explain—until *he* understood what the true situation was.

"Mom thinks you're with her. She called bright and early this morning to remind me to save anything left over from the wedding that you and Jo can use."

"I'm screwed." His mother didn't have a neutral setting. It was full speed ahead and that was all she wrote.

"I'd say." His brother lowered his voice. "You with Julie?"

Pat paused while staring at a row of toothbrushes and floss. "Yeah. I told her the truth."

"And?"

He hesitated. "And, this could end horribly for me."

"What is the truth, Pat?"

He assumed his brother already figured it out. "It's always been Julie. Jo and I..."

"You're just friends. I get it. I figured as much. But why the lie?"

"It's a pain being single and dealing with all the setups. It was the only way I could get Jo to come home."

"Say no more. I totally get it. What's up with Julie and Lance?"

"She says it's over but *complicated.*" His lips pressed tight. "She's...hurting."

Over the silence he could sense his brother's disapproval. "Do we have to pay old Lance a visit?"

"She says he didn't lay a hand on her, but he definitely messed with her head. She seems...fragile. She said she can't make any big decisions right now."

"Which is why you're scared."

"I'm not scared—"

"Pat, it's okay to want to protect yourself. She means a lot to you."

He let out a breath. "What do I do, Ry? Do I back off and let her figure it out herself or do I..." He swallowed, questioning if his motives were completely pure. "I don't want to take advantage of her in a fragile state."

"Julie's a smart girl. And even if she's feeling a little delicate right now, you would never intentionally hurt her. Trust yourself. Where are you?"

"The drug store. She wants to avoid people for a while."

"So, take her away. Maybe she needs a safe place and a friend right now. That's always been you."

He turned the corner and stopped short at the display of condoms. "What if things get…heated?"

"You mean like sex?" His brother laughed. "Then you fucking enjoy it, Pat. Christ, you waited your whole life for a shot with her, don't let guilt get in your way. If she said they're broken up, then they're broken up. Julie's a grown woman who can decide for herself what she wants. You're not a guy to pressure anyone, and you would never let yourself take advantage of her."

Pat grabbed a box and dropped it into the basket. "I don't think it will get that far."

"Well, if it does, I'm happy for you."

He blew out another breath. He was a mess. And as he unloaded the basket full of snacks, personal products, and condoms onto the checkout counter he was pretty sure the clerk thought he was high and up to no good.

"About today, I might have to—"

"Take as much time as you need. Deal with this."

He swiped his debit card and paid. "I feel like the worst best man ever."

"I think you're better than you realize. Just get to the alter on time and we're cool. Good luck with Julie."

"Thanks." He ended the call and grabbed his bags.

~

WHILE PAT WAS in the pharmacy, Julie lowered the visor, doing a quick inspection of her hair and what was left of her makeup. She rummaged through her purse for some gloss and a comb, only to come up short when she found her cellphone with nine-teen missed calls, two from Jo and the rest from Lance.

She sent her sister a quick text, telling her she was alive but needed time away from everything to think, then she shut off her phone. Pat returned with two bags and set them on the back seat.

She glanced at the bags, wondering what he bought when her eyes landed on a small box pressing against the transparent plastic. Condoms.

Her heart picked up pace as he headed back toward the mountains. "Where are we going?"

"Remember the cabin?"

"The little one in the woods we used to play at when we visited your cousin, Sheilagh?"

"Yeah."

She remembered. It was where Pat first told her he wanted to be a doctor. They had been swimming in the creek —something they weren't supposed to do without an adult— and she'd slipped on a mossy rock and cut her knee wide open.

Terrified that she might need stitches, they ran to the cabin hoping to find a first aid kit. Jo and Sheilagh played lookout while Pat patched up her knee. She still had the scar and her finger traced over the silver mark with fond nostalgia. Pat always took care of her when she needed it.

It took a while to get up the mountain, as her car was not made for off-road travel, and the trails leading up to the cabin were pocked with divots and puddles. When they finally reached the secluded hunting shack, it didn't quite match her memory.

The cabin looked smaller than she remembered. And nicer. "Someone's been here." There were two wooden rocking chairs on the small porch that looked freshly painted.

Pat carried the bags and found a hidden key above the door. Someone had definitely been using the cabin. The old futon cot had been replaced with a large bed, and the windows, which used to be covered with army green cloth, now had curtains.

"Someone's been *glamping,*" she said, opening the cabinets and finding them fully supplied with wine, canned food, dishes, and utensils. The fireplace was cleaned out and set with fresh logs and a bundle of twigs and cinnamon.

Pat followed her stare. "That's Tristan's trick. He and Luke must come here once in a while. The man loves burning spices on an open fire."

She smiled, thinking it completely romantic that they'd turned this little abandoned hideaway into some sort of love nest. "Will they be upset if we use it?"

"No, it belongs to all of us." He put the bags on the wooden table, and they stood in awkward silence.

"I'm gonna freshen up." She collected the toothbrush and toothpaste and disappeared in the small bathroom. When she returned, the items from the pharmacy were out of sight, and he was heating up a frying pan at the stove.

"What are you making?" she stood close to him, tempted to wrap her arms around his waist and rest her head on his back but unsure if that would be welcome.

"Bacon and eggs. I hope that's okay. They didn't have a lot of options at the store."

"Can I help?"

"Want to figure out the coffee pot?"

"Sure."

It was an old enamel percolator. While Pat took a moment to clean up, she packed the basket with grounds and hung it over from the spit in the fireplace. "This is so pretty it seems a shame to light it."

He snuck up behind her, surprising her by slipping his arms around her, much the way she'd wanted to slip her arms around him. "I want to make love to you in front of that fire, so it has to be done."

His directness shocked and excited her. She reached for the box of matches on the mantle and struck one, tossing it onto the arranged logs.

They watched its underwhelming landing and both laughed when it went out.

"Let me try." He bent to light the kindling and set the four corners of the arranged logs on fire. The flames caught and started to burn, the scent of cinnamon, smoke, and coffee mingling in the air.

"Fire's lit," she whispered, her own boldness as surprising as it was delightful.

Pat's arms closed around her and tightened. His lips pressed to the side of her neck. "Is that consent?"

"It's not a no."

What was she doing? Was this crazy? Three days ago, she was engaged and living with someone else. Was this what it felt like to throw caution to the wind and choose happiness, or was she self-sabotaging? Unsure, she broke contact and went to the stove.

"Julie?"

"Hmm?" She wanted him but didn't trust herself. Resentment boiled under the surface as she wondered if this was more of Lance's baggage. How long would she carry these doubts and second-guess the slightest decisions?

"You okay?"

She nodded and carefully turned the bacon.

"Hey."

Her shoulders tensed as he tucked her hair behind her ear. That was her only shelter at the moment and she wanted to hide behind it.

"Talk to me."

Placing the fork on the counter, she turned to face him. "I'm scared."

"Of me?"

"No, of me." She collected a dish rag from the counter and folded it, only to unfold it and fold it again.

"Do you want to leave?"

"No. I want to be here with you, with the fire and the… I want this."

"Then what is it?"

"I can't promise I'll want it tomorrow."

Something flashed in his eyes, but he blanked his expression, cutting her off from his usual transparency. "Okay."

"It's not because I don't like you, Pat. I do. But this has been a really long week after a really long confusing year, and I just don't want to lead you on."

"I get it."

She was a horrible person. She shouldn't involve him in her life when it was so uncertain. But a selfish part of her wanted to see what it might be like with him, even if it was just a glimpse at normal affection. Again, she questioned her decision-making. She trusted him more than she trusted herself right now, and maybe that was the allure.

Pat equaled safety. She hadn't felt safe in so long. She could finally let her guard down and just be herself. But this woman he revealed, she wasn't anyone she recognized. She wasn't timid or fearful. Did that make her dangerous?

Maybe such recklessness wouldn't necessarily hurt *her,* but what if it hurt Pat? She didn't want that to happen. Was her emotional whiplash getting to him? She glanced at him in question and winced at the uncertainty in his eyes. Maybe that was how normal people looked at crazy people.

"You're upset." She was trying to be honest, but there seemed no way around disappointing him. Once again, her insides twisted with guilt.

"Not upset, just trying to understand, and the bacon's burning." He carefully nudged her out of the way and transferred the strips onto a paper plate with a paper towel on top to absorb the grease.

"You're calmer than I remember."

"I guess you learn not to overreact when you work in an ER."

Good. Normal conversation. "Do you like being a doctor?" She watched him carefully crack the eggs into the pan.

"I do. But I prefer consistency, which is why I'd rather open my own practice. There would still be emergencies, but nothing as exciting as a big-city ER."

"Is that why you were looking at the bookstore?"

"Yes." He flipped the eggs.

"I think that could make a nice doctor's office."

"You do?" He looked at her like her opinion actually meant something to him.

"Sure. I mean, it's small, but this is a small town. You could make it really cute with the help of a good carpenter."

"That's what I think."

"Is there a second floor?"

"Yeah, but I'd use that as an apartment for now."

She smiled, impressed with how scaled back and simple he made it all seem. He was probably one of the most successful people from their graduating class. As a doctor, he could work anywhere. "Why did you come back here?"

His head cocked. "Why wouldn't I? This is where my family is."

"But you could have moved anywhere. Didn't you like the city?"

"I do, but I never wanted that long-term. I have other dreams."

She stole a piece of bacon and popped it in her mouth as he plated the eggs. "Like what?"

They sat at the table. The coffee had begun to perk and the cabin smelled amazing. "I want the private practice, the house, the yard, the chocolate lab, the picket fence…the wife."

Who didn't want all those things? "Well, it looks like you're almost there."

"Almost."

They ate and he asked her about her time in Maryland, but she didn't have much to share. "I worked for a while for a paralegal, but I wasn't really qualified for the job, so I left."

He frowned. "Don't you have your bachelor's degree?"

"Yes, but it's in business administration."

He looked even more confused. "I thought that was more than enough to be a paralegal. Is Maryland different?"

"Oh, I wasn't the acting paralegal. I just handled the office administrator stuff."

"Wait, so you were doing something that you had college training to do?"

"Yes, but…" It was more complicated than that. "I wasn't cut out for the work. I…"

His hand covered hers. "Julie, you wouldn't have a diploma if you weren't qualified to do that sort of work. Whoever told you otherwise, underestimated you."

She poked at her food, no longer hungry. "It doesn't matter anymore anyway. After I left, I never went back."

"So, what did you do?"

She scoffed. "Laundry. I shopped for household items I didn't need. I made projects out of organizing closets and the pantry and anything else I could do to fill up my days. With no kids, it gets a little boring being home alone."

"Do you want kids?"

She used to dream about being a mother, but she'd been so concerned about her mental state lately and the circumstances at home, she now worried that dream might be unwise. The more Lance revealed his true self, the more she worried about his parenting qualifications. But it wasn't just Lance she worried about. The thought of being responsible for others right now, terrified her. "I don't know if I'd be a good mother."

"What are you talking about? You'd be a great mom. You're patient and kind and funny. If you want kids, don't let doubt slow you down."

She thought about her own mother, who lived within the strict confines of her faith and only spoke in terms of worries and setbacks. It was amazing they weren't more screwed up. "I can't think about kids right now. I can barely take care of myself."

"Hey, you'll get back on your feet. Just give it time."

She appreciated his confidence. "Thanks. I hope you're right."

"How about we find some thermoses, grab some coffee, and go on an adventure like old times?"

She looked down at her dress. "I'm not really dressed for a hike."

He pointed to the wall where a shelf hung. Plaid flannel and gray cotton folded in a stack. "What about shoes?"

He glanced under the table at her flats. "That might be an issue. What if we take it slow and stick to the trail?"

"That should be fine."

After breakfast, she changed while Pat did the dishes and made up the thermoses of coffee. She emerged from the bathroom and couldn't stop laughing. If this ensemble was supposed to tempt a man, boy had she been doing it wrong all these years.

When he turned and first spotted her, his eyes widened, his gaze stroking slowly from her head to toes. She'd pulled her hair into a messy bun and tied the oversized flannel at her ribs. The pants were several sizes too big, so she rolled them at her waist and cuffed the extra material at her ankles. With her ballet flats, she was certain she looked ridiculous.

"You look like a magic genie. If I rub you, do I get three wishes?"

"Depends what you ask for."

His brows shot up. "I'll have to think about that."

They walked the trail beside the creek and saw some trout along the way. At the falls they looked for bear but didn't see any. They did spot a few deer, but nothing was cuter than the chipmunks scurrying about the roots and boulders.

"How are your feet holding up?"

She looked down at her delicate shoes, resigned to this being the last time she'd wear them. Her feet were starting to hurt. "They've been better."

"Then we should head back."

When they walked over an uneven patch of ground, he took her arm so she wouldn't fall. Pat had always been thoughtful of others, but there was something different about the way he treated her now. He was careful with her and always checking in with little questions, like if the sun was getting to her or if she needed to rest.

Lance was never that attentive. And if she ever complained about any form of discomfort, he usually acted like she was making a big deal out of nothing. Come to think of it, she'd become a bit of a liar, stuffing down the littlest complaint so it didn't come back and bite her in the ass later. He was notorious for throwing things in her face long after-the-fact.

It was refreshing to spend an afternoon with Pat. He didn't complain or point out what she was doing wrong. He was polite and helpful. He smiled easily, and he made her smile, too.

By the time they returned to the cabin, the sun had hit its high point and she was overheated. She sat outside on the rocking chair, giving her feet much needed rest. Peeling off her ruined little shoes, which had gotten caked with mud, she winced at the sting of a blister forming.

The screen door opened and Pat appeared with two glasses of water. "Ouch. Let me see that."

"It's fine." She dropped her foot and took the water.

He pulled the other chair across from her and set his glass on the rail. "Julie, let me see your foot."

"I'm not showing you my feet. I need a pedicure."

Ignoring her, he reached forward and yanked her foot onto his lap. "It's red. And it looks like you have a blister starting."

"I'm really self-conscious about my feet."

"Relax, you. I'm a doctor. There isn't a part of the human body that can freak me out at this point." He pressed his thumbs into her arch, and the overworked muscles and tendons relaxed. "Feel good?"

It felt so good her eyes started to roll back. "Did they teach that in medical school?"

"I took a reflexology course. Did you know there's a place on the foot that can hit almost any nerve in the body?"

"I think you're hitting my narcolepsy nerve, because you're about to put me to sleep."

He continued to massage. "This area releases tension."

"I can tell."

"And this…" He dragged a finger down the arch of her foot, tickling her but not letting go. "This area connects to the nerves in your back."

"Whoa!" She felt something buzz along her spine. "Do something else."

"This works your eyes." He tugged her second smallest

toe, and she felt a strange loosening of tension around her face. "And this is your sinuses."

"That's so cool. I can feel it."

"How about this?" He pressed hard on the inner heel near the bottom of her foot and her eyes widened.

"Hey!" She felt something tighten in her lower regions.

He laughed. "Too much?" He moved his massaging fingers higher between her arch and ankle bone, and pressed. "How about now?"

"Stop that!" She could feel things happening around her girlie parts. "How is that even possible?"

He chuckled and went back to what seemed like a normal foot massage. "I think you have nice feet."

She peeked through her lashes, watching him. He was totally unbothered. "Did you really have a crush on me as long as you said?"

"Yes."

"Why didn't you ever say anything?"

He shrugged and continued massaging. "You're intimidating. I mean, look at how you dress."

She smirked. "Smart-ass."

"Give me your other foot."

Without hesitating, she replaced her left foot with her right. "I would have said yes, if you would have asked me out."

He didn't look up or respond.

She realized then what it must have done to him, seeing her with Lance all those years. "Did you hate him because I was with him, or did you hate that I was with someone like him?"

"Both. You were always too good for him. But, even without you, I would have disliked him. He's a dick."

She'd grown so used to Lance constantly reminding her how many people liked and admired him, it was strange to remember that wasn't always true. Maybe it was hardly ever true. "Do other people dislike him?"

"Your sister hates him."

"Jo? No, she doesn't."

He raised an eyebrow, challenging her. *Did* Jo hate Lance? Maybe that was why she stopped hanging out with them, and why she eventually moved away.

"What about Sheilagh?"

He sighed and sat back, no longer massaging but retaining a hold of her foot on his lap. "Aside from the shitty way he treated you, few people liked him. He's insecure and always overcompensating. It's hard to listen to that after a while."

"You think Lance is insecure?"

"Absolutely."

She frowned, having a hard time qualifying him as such. He always carried himself with such unbending certainty at home. "And you think he treated me shitty? Even before the things I told you last night?"

"I remember one time in high school we all went out for milkshakes. You kept talking about how much you were craving a mint chocolate chip shake, but when we got there, Lance ordered you a vanilla shake. You told him it wasn't what you wanted—and we all heard you say you wanted mint—but he gave you a bunch of crap about changing your mind and being difficult."

"I don't remember that. I guess he did stuff like that so much I stopped keeping track." She didn't want to talk about Lance anymore.

His hand rubbed over the top of her foot, trailing along her ankle. "How about I use one of my wishes?"

Whatever she'd been thinking, his question sidetracked her. A flush heated her cheeks and she smiled. "What do you want?"

"Everything you're willing to offer."

The breath vanished from her lungs. "You're dangerous, Patrick."

"Nah, I'm just your old childhood friend, Pat."

"Little Pat never looked at me the way you're looking at me now."

"How am I looking at you?"

"Like you want to swallow me whole."

His mouth curved with a half smile. "I've spent my entire life looking at you like this, Jules, but only when you were focused on something else. I'm done hiding."

"See? Dangerous."

"Why dangerous? Why not upfront or direct?"

"You're those things, too. But you're mostly dangerous, because you make me want to say yes to whatever you ask."

His eyes seemed to darken. "Would that be such a crime?"

She honestly didn't know. "I don't want to lose you."

He frowned. "I'm not going anywhere."

"I know. But if I stay here, I'll need a friend. Sheilagh's a mom and wife now. She's busy. And Jo's going back to Philly after the wedding."

"I'll always be your friend, Julie."

"Promise?"

He nodded. "Promise."

She dragged her feet off his lap and stood.

"Where are you going?"

"Inside."

"And what happens inside?"

She pulled open the door and glanced back at him. "Whatever you want."

CHAPTER 10

Julie crossed the threshold, but the door didn't slam, as Pat caught it behind her. "Where did you hide the condoms?"

"We'll get to that."

"But I want to make sure we—"

He silenced her with a deep, soul rattling kiss and backed her to the bed, lowering her onto the tartan coverlet. "I'll always protect you, Julie. Don't worry about the technicalities. I got this." He straddled her hips and sat up, giving the flannel shirt a tug under her breasts where she'd knotted it. "Can I take this off?"

Staring up at Pat, she found him so attractive, she again wondered why she never let herself see him in such a light before. Maybe she never thought *this* could be possible. But here they were and it felt so…easy to give in.

Her arms opened and fell to the side. "You can take it all off. I told you. You can have everything you want."

"Does that offer have an expiration date?"

She swallowed, wishing she could offer him a guarantee.

"Let's just live in the present, Patrick. That's as far as I can think right now."

"Then I better make it count." He tugged the shirt and it loosened. Button after button, he slowly parted the fabric, exposing her bare breasts. Scooting low, he caressed her flesh and kissed her nipples into hard peaks.

When he touched her, he did so with such attention to detail, she grew self-conscious like she might be taking too long. Guiding his hand lower, he twisted out of her grip and caught her wrist, pressing it into the bedding.

"Patience."

His body grew hard, and as he kissed and touched her, she became hot with need. Maybe he'd want her to touch him.

"Do you want…my mouth."

He paused and glanced down at her. "I want *all* of you."

She nodded, still unsure if he would want other things. Insecurity knifed through her. Lance had a way of doing things. He'd come home after a stressful day and tell her he didn't need her to talk, he needed her to use her mouth in other ways.

"Hey." Pat caught her chin, and her vision focused. "What just happened?"

Her cheeks burned but not in a good way. Tears stung the backs of her eyes. She hated that Lance was all she knew. She turned away, pulling her chin from his grip.

"Julie, talk to me. Is there something you want?"

"No," she all but choked on the word. Lance never asked what she wanted, when it came to this. The thought of trying to verbalize her own desires left her uneasy and nervous.

"Then what?"

Her limited experience, after being with one person for so long, was too humiliating to explain. She could see *him* using her all those times, treating her like an empty vessel. If she ever voiced the slightest complaint, he'd say she was cold and remind her that other women *liked* having sex.

It wasn't that she didn't like it. It just felt one-sided a lot of times. He showed her videos of other women doing the things he wanted.

"See, they like it," he'd say, and she'd think to herself that those women were actors who got paid to act like they enjoyed anything.

"Maybe just not as rough," she suggested one time, and he went on a rant about rough being code for passion.

"Have a little fun for once," Lance had said to that, and she reminded him it wasn't fun if she felt like she couldn't breathe. But he didn't acknowledge her discomfort as anything more than an obstacle *she* needed to work through.

She'd gotten better at it over time, more tolerant. But she *never* looked forward to it. Sometimes he'd ask for it as soon as he walked through the door, which was fine, because she'd do it and it would be over.

He never forced her, but on the days she made excuses, he fell into an ominous mood that seemed to suck the air out of the house. She realized, despite all the things she'd done to please him, he still remained disappointed with her lack of enthusiasm on most days.

What if Pat was also disappointed?

Pat rolled off of her and closed her shirt. "Julie, you have to talk to me. I'm getting mixed signals here, and I don't know what happened."

Her body had gone cold, and any sign of arousal had disappeared the moment thoughts of Lance intruded in her mind. She covered her eyes with her hand. "I think… I'm more messed up than I realized."

"What do you mean?"

She didn't think being with Pat would trigger her like this. And to be honest, it wasn't Pat. It was the situation that was triggering her. She wanted him to keep looking at her like she was special. No one had made her feel special in so long, she didn't want to screw it up by not living up to his expectations. "I just want you to know I'm willing to do anything you need. I don't want to disappoint you."

"Disappoint me? Jules, I don't need you to do *anything.* I just want to be with you. And if we can't do that, then we don't and we move on. Trust me. You can't disappoint me."

"I just thought..."

"What? That I needed something *extra*?" He took her hand and pressed it to his lap. "You've already got me, sweetheart. No extra effort necessary."

Lance was so specific in bed. He had so many strange requests and would often critique her performance afterwards, giving her tips about how she could make it better. What if she was just bad in bed and Lance was actually being incredibly patient all these years?

Her head hurt from thinking, and she pinched the bridge of her nose.

"Hey, we can stop. We can just relax and talk."

But she wanted to be with him. She just had to be honest with him, even if talking about this mortified her. "I...I don't know anything aside from the things he taught me, and I'm getting the sense he kept me misinformed on purpose."

Understanding flashed in his eyes, quickly followed by fury. "I see." He spoke as if he were afraid to say more.

"Please don't be mad at me—"

"I'm not mad at you. But if I'm understanding you correctly, I'd like to murder Lance." He got off the bed and paced. "Without going into too much detail, how much did you learn from him?"

"All of it. My mom thinks it's a husband's job to teach his wife, and she refuses to acknowledge that I'm living in sin. And Jo never liked talking about boys. Lance never minded telling me what to do, but… I didn't care for a lot of the things he liked."

"I'm imagining some really bad shit right now, Julie. How off do you think I am?"

"I don't know."

The muscles in his jaw flexed. "How often did you two…"

"Every day. Sometimes twice a day, but it wasn't always sex. Most of the time it was me just—"

"Okay." He held up his hands. "Sorry. I get the picture." He paced some more. "Was he gentle?"

"Never with that."

When he exhaled, she heard the shakiness of his breath. He went to the cabinets and pulled down a bottle of wine. Then searched the drawers for a bottle opener. Once he had the bottle uncorked, he drank right from the mouth.

"Here's what's gonna happen." He returned to pacing and he suddenly seemed so much more powerful and intimidating than the little Patrick Clooney she used to know. But strangely, she wasn't afraid of him. If anything, the bigger and more commanding he appeared the safer he made her feel, like he would only ever use his size and strength to protect her. "I need a few minutes to clear my head. Why don't you take a shower and relax? There are towels on the shelf."

"Do you regret bringing me here?"

"No, but I regret ever letting you leave with him."

"You couldn't have stopped me. He can be charming."

"Julie, I can bear a lot, but I can't bear you defending him. At least not right now."

She didn't say it to defend Lance. "I'm only saying that so you don't think I'm stupid. I'd never get involved with someone who treated me the way he did at his worst. I know he can be a monster at times, but he's other things, too. I know who he is, and I know he has bad sides, but those aren't the sides he showed me in the beginning. It's important to me that you know that."

He put down the bottle and crossed the cabin, cupping her face and looking her right in the eye. "Listen to me. I know you're not stupid. Anyone who thinks you are, is an idiot and doesn't know you. I understand how manipulation works, and I get that he didn't change overnight. I'd never blame you for being with him. I just wish I could have saved you any suffering he caused. If anything, I blame myself."

Pat seemed to hold a clearer picture in his mind of the strong-willed girl she used to be than she currently held. Her vision blurred as she smiled at him, truly appreciating his ability to understand how complicated this was for her. He was like a guiding light in a storm. He made her believe she'd eventually find her way back to the person she was.

She scooted off the bed and closed her hand around his, her gratitude for his patience clogging her throat and her gaze pleading with him never to change.

"I'm glad you brought me here, Pat." He stilled from pacing and stared down at her. When he looked at her like that, like she was the most precious woman in the world, she felt capable of anything. "I still want to be with you tonight."

His hand gently cupped the side of her face, but she sensed his tension. "Then give me ten minutes. Please."

She nodded and traced his hand with hers before turning away. When she reached the small bathroom and glanced back, his back was rigid under his shirt, and for once, he wasn't looking at her.

Uncertainty teased the pit of her stomach, but she did as he asked. She gave him time and space to process, praying she hadn't just destroyed this delicate new thing they shared.

Patrick had always been in her life—until he wasn't. It felt right having him back. But it also felt like so much more had come with him. He awakened something inside of her, something that scared and excited her, something that made her feel safe and a little reckless.

As she stood under the spray of the water, some of her tension washed away and she started to relax, not from the heat or the steam, but from the promise of knowing Patrick waited just outside for her. It was then that she realized how much she wanted him—in her life and in her future. Perhaps even *needed* him, as he seemed the only one capable of mending the broken bits of her heart and making her feel like a decent and deserving woman again.

It wasn't something he did or anything he gave her, but somehow he restored her belief in herself. She needed that. She needed to believe that she was worth loving, that she was deserving of kindness, no matter what mistakes she'd made.

But she still didn't fully trust her judgement, and reality was a lot different than a hidden cabin in the woods. Part of her wished they could stay hidden there forever.

CHAPTER 11

Pat was going to pulverize Lance if he ever saw him again. The images rushing through his mind were so disturbing he couldn't catch his breath. Adrenaline pumped through his veins as he stood on the porch, the fresh air doing little to calm his rage. Why had it never occurred to him that she would be so inexperienced?

It made perfect sense. Her mother had a warped sense of old world values even he couldn't comprehend. Once, Jo told him her mother forbade them to use tampons because nothing but a husband and the Holy Spirit should go inside a woman. Of course Mrs. Cook wouldn't educate her daughters about sex.

And Lance knew that. He knew what kind of home Julie grew up in and used her ignorance to his advantage. Pat could only imagine the sort of depraved things he convinced her to do.

It would break him if she took that selfish bastard back. He could deal with her moving on and he could accept it if she didn't want him. But she deserved to be happy and she deserved a relationship based on trust and honesty. She'd never find that with Lance.

A floorboard creaked and he turned, finding Julie behind him, looking small and innocent as she stood in a towel. She'd left her hair up, but a few runaway strands had fallen loose and curled from the steam.

He stared at her through the screen door, wondering if he could even be the sort of man she deserved. He'd try his best.

He shut the door behind him and lowered the blinds. "Do you want a glass of wine?"

"I'm okay right now."

He set the bottle aside. He didn't approach her, because he hadn't yet thought of how he wanted to do this. Turned out, he didn't have to.

Julie dropped the towel and slowly crossed the cabin. "Is this okay?"

Her pebbled nipples pressed to his chest as she raised her arms to his shoulders and lifted to her toes, rising for a kiss. He'd meant to be the one in control, but this brazen beauty seemed to disarm him of his senses every time.

"I don't want to think about anything but us right now," she whispered, nudging her nose along his jaw. "I don't want you to think of me anywhere but here—with you."

His throat and pants tightened and he swallowed hard. His fingers framed her bare waist and he stared into her eyes. A million unspoken promises rushed through his head. She would always be able to trust him. He'd never hurt her. He'd always be gentle with her.

Was his silence another truth? Even he, with all of his good intentions and affection for her, could not promise such things, because love didn't come with guarantees. And neither could she make those promises to him, but he wanted her anyway.

His lips grazed her cheek and he whispered, "Just us, right now."

Dear God, he hoped this didn't destroy him. As she pressed closer, he lifted her, pulling her legs around his waist and deepening the kiss. His hands dragged down her spine, tracing the delicate line and cupping her soft ass.

It didn't take long for his tension to unwind. Carrying her to the bed, he gently placed her beneath him, taking his time to explore her curves with kisses and soft nibbles. She was so responsive, eager, and accommodating.

As he softly stroked silken skin, he nudged her knees further apart, fitting his shoulders between her fallen thighs. He kissed a trail down her stomach and bit softly at her hip. Spreading her folds open, he found her little jewel and pressed a kiss there.

Her body tensed, so he whispered and soothed her. Slow, tender licks left her shaking, but soon she was moaning and trembling when his caresses felt especially pleasurable. If Lance had been as selfish in bed as he was in everything else, chances are he rarely took care of her this way.

Pat got lost in her flavor and scent. Her delicate almost tentative response grew more confident the longer he took his time, and soon she was quivering and crying out his name. He brought her to climax again and again, sometimes rapidly, sometimes slowly, but always completely.

Pulling his clothes off, he reached under the pillows for the box of condoms. She watched him, not missing a beat as he stripped off his briefs and stroked himself. Their gazes met, and she smiled, then surprised him by taking the condom from him and placing a kiss on his shaft.

She was exploratory and gentle. He waited and enjoyed every attentive kiss. When she took him into her mouth, his fingers traced slow swirls over her bare shoulders as he gave her complete control.

"Do you like that?" she looked up at him, seeking reassurance, and it nearly broke him.

Dragging a thumb over her full lower lip, he smiled at her. "I love everything you do."

She smiled back and lowered her head again. She nearly finished him, but he lifted her for a deep kiss, rolling her to her back. He slid down the condom and aligned his body with hers, staring into her eyes.

"I've imagined this a million different ways, but it's never come close to the reality."

Her hand traced along the stubble at his jaw and she smiled. "Show me how it's supposed to be."

He slid forward and they both gasped at the incredible sensation. Her nails dug into his muscled flesh, and he kept his gaze on her. He kissed her hungrily, showing her how endless his desire for her was.

Her body gripped his and trembled when he pressed deep, stroking that sensitive spot inside a woman, where the earth meets heaven. Her body bowed and she called his name, urging him faster in a storm of desire and pent-up lust. She rocked his soul and unraveled knots in him that had been tied for decades. He was flying and falling, existing in a place with no darkness or time, only pleasure and his beautiful Julie. When they finished together, he felt rewritten as a man, certain that no other woman could ever come close to her in his heart.

The intensity of their connection was sewn by a friendship that was more than twenty years old. They knew each other's secrets and fears. He could recall the cause of almost every scar on her body and knew what she sounded like when she laughed her hardest and unfortunately, what she sounded like when she cried. Experiencing this intimate part of her, closed something in him that had been left open and suffering too long. This linked them tighter than they ever were before.

Clinging tight to one another, she smiled at him and whispered, “I could so easily fall in love with you.”

He wanted that more than his next breath. “I’ve already fallen, so I’ll be waiting to catch you whenever you’re ready.”

CHAPTER 12

Spending the day with Pat was like hiding away in the soft safety of a cloud or the sapphire curl of a wave. No one could reach them there, and they were free to be whoever they wanted. Pat made her feel safe to be herself, as if the woman she'd become was the perfect mix of flaws and rightness. He made her like herself again, and she hadn't liked herself in a very long time.

"Okay, Mr. Murdock—current age—Old Man McGinty, and Father Mark."

Julie rolled on her back, covering her face with her palms and laughing. "No, I can't!"

"You have to!" Pat draped his upper body over her bare belly, cheek pressed to her skin and hands casually exploring.

She'd slipped the flannel back on because the cabin air caught a chill once the sun set, but they were still mostly naked. The crunch of a cheese puff broke the silence as he chewed.

She held out a hand, and he placed three light orange balls in her palm. She munched as she thought. "Mr. Murdock, our environmental science teacher?"

"Yep!"

"The one with the toupee?"

"You can have him keep it on or take it off. It's your fantasy."

She pegged him in the forehead with an orange cheese puff. "*This* is not my fantasy. This is mean."

"You have to pick."

"Fine." She groaned. "I guess I'd marry Old Man McGinty, fuck Father Mark, and kill poor Mr. Murdock."

Pat gasped dramatically. "You dirty little harlot. You'd fuck the priest?"

"He's the youngest! The other two are crypt keepers."

"Ageist and a sinner. Okay."

She giggled. "Maybe a little bit of a gold digger, too. I'd inherit McGinty's fortune and become the Queen merchant of all of Jasper Falls."

Shaking his head in mock disapproval, he tsked. "Shameless."

She stretched and brushed the orange crumbs off her fingers. "It feels good to act shamelessly for once. I'm so tired of always trying to do what other people expect of me or worse, trying to guess what they want."

He turned to face her. "Then don't. Just be yourself. If someone doesn't like it, they don't have to be around you. But the people who stick by your side… You'll know they genuinely love you."

Her smile softened. "Have you always been this sweet?"

"When it comes to you? Probably."

"Why me? Never mind." She didn't want to seem needy or make him think she was fishing for compliments. But she *was* needy at the moment, and fragile, and he was repairing so many of her broken parts, she was getting greedy.

He stared at her, his eyes holding a world of secrets she

wanted to unravel. “I don’t know. You were always just…nice to me.”

“Were other people mean to you?” She didn’t recall Pat ever getting bullied.

He shrugged, and his gaze shifted to the fire. “No, not with Ryan and all my older cousins around. But I knew where I ranked on the totem pole.”

“What do you mean?” Her heart pinched at the thought of others overlooking him. Had she been one of them? She always thought they had a genuine friendship. And if she had known his feelings, she surely wouldn’t have made some of the decisions she had.

He shrugged. “I was the scrawny kid with red hair, glasses, and freckles. And my acne days were a real treat. Guys overlooked me and girls looked through me.”

“I never looked through you, Patrick.”

He met her stare with something challenging in his green eyes, and she accepted that perhaps she had. She’d been oblivious to his feelings up until this week. Guilt washed over her.

“It’s fine.” He turned his head again to watch the fire.

But it wasn’t fine. It made her feel like a bad friend. “I saw you, Patrick. I remember almost every single time you and I were alone. I might not have known your feelings, but I knew how you made me feel. I was always safe with you. I could trust you, count on you. Aside from Jo, who was always closer to Sheilagh, you were probably my closest friend growing up. And when you cut me off… I felt it.”

He turned his head, to say something but rather, rose and kissed her. “I’m sorry. I never meant to hurt you.”

It was such a soft, genuine kiss, as if it wasn’t a kiss at all but a delicate truth he couldn’t undo. Lance never kissed her like that—or apologized.

Her fingers stroked the stubble at his jaw, and she smiled,

in awe of the man he'd become. "For the record, I always loved your red hair and freckles. And I thought your glasses made you look smart."

When he kissed again her, it was with purpose. It didn't take long for him to find his way back inside of her.

That night they made love several times in front of the fire, just as he promised. In between kissing and fooling around, they talked and rummaged through the cabinets. As midnight approached, she suffered a sort of Cinderella dread, like the dream might suddenly end and all of this magic would be ripped away. She wanted to stay hidden in the woods with him as long as she could.

"We can stay until morning," he whispered, softly stroking her hair as they spooned, facing the hypnotic fire.

"Okay." She had nothing to do and wanted nothing more than to stay hidden away from the world, wrapped in the safety of his arms.

He kissed her ear then pulled the covers over her shoulder. "Try to get some sleep."

But she didn't sleep. She stayed up most the night, listening to his steady breathing, wondering what her future might look like, and savoring the sensation of being held safely by a friend.

CHAPTER 13

"Where the hell have you been?" his mother shrilled. "I've had half the town out looking for you! Your brother is getting married tomorrow, and you're supposed to be his best man!"

"I'm fine, Mum," Ryan said, pouring a cup of coffee. "Everything's handled. Hey, Pat."

"Hey, man." As soon as Pat returned home, his mother threw a fit and had been lecturing him ever since. Another reason why he might take that bookstore rather than wait for something better to come along.

"Now, I'll have to make a hundred calls to tell everyone you're not lying in a ditch somewhere."

He rolled his eyes. When she said she involved half the town in a search party, that really meant she called the aunts and they asked his fifty cousins if anyone had seen him. "Just call Aunt Maureen and tell her I'm home now." The woman could spread news faster than wildfire.

"That's not the point! Where were you? I called Josephine, and she was rather short with me."

He could imagine. She was another one he needed to talk

to. He wished he could be a fly on the wall in her house, because Julie was likely speaking to her right now. "Don't bring Jo into this."

"Why not? She's your fiancée."

"About that—"

"Rosemarie!" His father called from the front door. "Who the hell left these boxes all over the front porch? It stinks to high heaven out here!"

His mother rushed to the front door and unleashed a string of vulgar profanity. "I told them to deliver to the tavern. The house was the billing address, not the shipping address! Ryan, Patrick, go get the truck. We have a hundred pounds of fish to move."

Pat frowned. "Fish?"

His brother cursed and dumped his coffee. "Great."

The fish was salmon, and it was for the wedding. Apparently it was supposed to go to O'Malley's, where the reception would be held, after a ceremony at the lake on McCullough Mountain.

"Ry, you should ask for a refund. By the time we get this loaded and unloaded, it will have been baking in the sun for over an hour. The guests will get sick."

"Oh, this is the last time I take advice from Colleen." His mother was already dialing, but he knew she wasn't calling the distributor. "Your back-alley fish dealer has my whole street stinking like a medieval brothel on an August day, Colleen!"

Aunt Colleen's voice shrilled on the other end. His mother took the call inside, blaming her sister for the mix-up in true family fashion, where they never let anyone off the hook without a little culpability.

He looked at Ryan who seemed overly stressed compared to his calm demeanor ten minutes ago. "Should we load this up?"

"It's all gotta go in the trash. We'll never get it on ice in time." He flipped open a cardboard lid and drew back. The stink of bad fish wafted through the air and was already permeating the paper packaging.

"Let's take it to the landfill. We can't put it in the dumpster. It'll have the whole town reeking tomorrow for the wedding."

The morning was spoiled by transporting rotting fish across town and trying to find a replacement dish for the guests within twenty-four hours. Luckily, Maggie used to work at Restaurant Supply, and they had enough meat on hand for Ryan to improvise.

"So, how was it?" Ryan asked on their trek back across town to drop off the meat order.

Pat didn't need his brother to specify that he was asking about Julie. "Did you ever imagine something perfect, like *absolutely* perfect, and the reality is so much better it makes the fantasy look flat and pale in hindsight?"

Ryan grinned and raised a brow as he turned onto Main Street. "*That* good?"

"Better."

He parked at the back of O'Malley's. "So, what now?"

A knot formed in Pat's gut. "I don't know. She's gotta straighten some stuff out and get settled. I want to go pack up her belongings in Maryland for her so it's done, but I can't. This is something she has to see through for herself."

"That sucks. She was with him for a long time. It has to be complicated as hell to break up a long relationship like that."

"I wouldn't know."

Ryan chuckled. "Me neither." He shut off the car and they waited in the AC before stepping into the hot summer air. "Do you think we're lucky? I mean, I always thought I was cursed because my entire dating life was a revolving door of fix ups, one night stands, and shitty blind dates. But then I found Maggie and it just feels different. Permanent. I can't imagine ever being with someone else."

Pat envied his brother but also felt incredibly happy for him. "I think that makes you the luckiest man in the world."

He gave him a knowing look. "You're lucky too, Pat. I've got a good feeling about this Julie thing. Not sure how you're going to explain it to the town when everyone thinks you're engaged to her sister, but it'll all work out." He cracked the door and hopped out.

On account of all the meat that needed to thaw, the kitchen at the pub had to close. They were working against the clock and short of fridge space.

"Who's cooking all of this?" Pat asked as the volume of the unpacked order overwhelmed the counterspace.

In their family it was tradition for the aunts to pull together and cook for family events, but meat took a lot more work than fish. Someone would be standing over a hot oven all day.

"Italian Mary's making trays of ziti and Aunt Col is doing the green beans. Aunt Maureen's doing the potatoes, and Anthony's sisters are doing the dessert trays. Uncle Paulie was supposed to do the main dishes."

It wouldn't be so bad if they didn't have a family the size of an army. "We really need a chef for things like this."

"Can you call Reggie?"

Ryan slammed another slab of beef onto the counter and pans rattled below. "No, an old loyalist like Reg can't overlook the O'Malley brawl from the seventies. He lost hearing in his left ear on that fateful day and he never got over it."

Pat rolled his eyes. "Those old farts really need to let that rivalry go. And Maggie is only an O'Malley by marriage. Plus, she won't be one for long."

Ryan grinned. "I can't wait to call her Mrs. Clooney." He

unpacked another slab of frozen meat from the box. "But regardless, Reggie's pretty settled into retirement now."

"What about Sue?" Sue, the steady bartender, knew how to do just about anything where O'Malley's was concerned since she'd worked there for years.

"She's been handling most of the cooking and complaining about it regularly. Every day she reminds Maggie she's *not* a cook, so there's no way she'd help with the wedding food. Plus, she's a guest."

"So is Uncle Paulie." It would inevitably be the Uncles grilling.

"That's better than a female guest. Girls get their hair done and wear nice dresses. It's one thing having the aunts toss fish in the oven, but we need someone to babysit the grill to make sure it's not overdone."

It looked like this one would fall on the men. Ryan called Uncle Frank, begging for some culinary aide, and the cavalry assembled, ready to assist Paulie with all the meat. The uncles and cousins broke the prep time into shifts and had it all figured out by two in the afternoon. In the end, they were only an hour late for their appointment with the tailor.

Once they had their final fittings and tux jackets in hand, they had to swing over to Aunt Colleen's to get their kilts.

"Don't touch anything, boys. I have a system." The entire living room was filled with Irish tartan, each kilt freshly pressed and marked with a strip of masking tape, labeling who it belonged to. "Ryan, I pressed your socks too."

The whole house smelled delicious. Pat took a detour into the kitchen, where he found Italian Mary hunched over a vat of meat sauce as she ladled it into mason jars.

He kissed her cheek and she smiled up at him. "Smells incredible."

She put down the ladle and waved a knotty finger at him.

"Here. You try." She took a slice of bread from a nearby bag, slathered soft butter on top and dipped it into the sauce.

His eyes rolled back in his head as the flavor melted in his mouth. "Delicious."

"I make a jar of gravy special for you."

He gratefully accepted the gift.

When they had their kilts and were on their way, Ryan glared at the souvenir of gravy. "How come you get sauce?"

"She likes me better, I guess."

"Italian Mary doesn't like anyone. And I'm the groom. If anyone should be getting special sauce, it should be me."

Pat snickered at his brother's jealousy. He didn't see the need to tell him the sauce was likely repayment for the CBD cream he'd sent Italian Mary to help with her arthritic hands. "Not everyone likes you best, Ry."

"Shut up."

It was after seven when they finally had most of the preparations made and the cars loaded for tomorrow. Ryan wanted to see Maggie one last time, since they wouldn't be spending the night before the wedding together, so he met her in town for a quiet dinner. This gave Pat the perfect opportunity to sneak away and see Julie.

"I'll be back, Mum." He grabbed his keys and opened the door, only to come up short when he found Jo about to knock on the other side. "What are you doing here?"

"I need to talk to you."

"I was just running out."

"No, you *weren't*." She grabbed his sleeve, dragging him back into the house and into his childhood bedroom, not stopping until she shut the door. She scowled at him and hissed, "You slept with my sister?"

He missed the part where this might be a problem—or her business. "Jo…"

"What about taking things slow? Seriously, Patrick, I thought you were smarter than that."

He frowned. "What's that supposed to mean? And, I've waited my entire life to be with her. How much slower can I go?"

"She literally *just* broke up with Lance. He's still blowing up her phone. Why would you get involved in that?"

"They're over."

"I hope so, but she's not over their relationship. He messed her up."

"I know. We talked about it. She told me everything."

"Oh, really?"

He got defensive. "Yes. Don't act like you're the only person she confides in. We spent the whole night talking." When she gave him a skeptical look, he added, "In between other things."

"Then you know."

He paused, backtracking and trying to figure out exactly what she was talking about. He believed Julie told him everything. What made Jo automatically assume she'd be more informed than him?

"I know everything you know, so stop acting like you have a better grip on the situation than me!"

Jo fisted her hands at her hips and leveled him with an unimpressed stare. "Then she told you she's pregnant?"

CHAPTER 14

Someone could have knocked him over with a feather. Chills raced under his skin, slipping over the surface of his blood as if it had frozen to a sheet of ice. He couldn't breathe. His lungs tightened, until it truly felt like he was drowning.

"What?" he wheezed.

"I knew you didn't know. She's pregnant with Lance's baby. So, knowing my sister and the hold this guy has on her, chances are, she'll take him back."

His legs gave out and he dropped to sit on the edge of his bed. "Why didn't she tell me?"

Jo sat beside him. "She's confused and scared. I know, in your head, the last day was like a dream come true, but to her, it wasn't about you. It was about her. I think you helped her, but you..." Jo squeezed his hand. "I'm sorry, Pat."

He couldn't figure out which way was up and which way was down. "I need to see Julie."

"Pat, you need to give her time to figure this out. She has to make the decision on her own."

"She doesn't trust her decision-making right now!"

"All the more reason to let her figure it out. Give her space. You and I both know she's able to decide for herself what she wants."

But what if she wanted Lance? What if she wanted to go back, not for her, but for the child's sake?

"Two days ago, you were so certain she was done with him."

Regret reflected in her eyes. "I didn't know about the baby then. I'm so sorry."

He frowned. "She made sure we were safe."

"Because she wanted to make sure you didn't think she was trying to manipulate you in any way. It's early. Lance doesn't even know yet."

"Does she plan on telling him?"

Jo's brows lifted. "You know her as well as anyone. Julie's always been honest to a fault."

Yet, she didn't tell Pat she was pregnant. Maybe she was still processing. "I don't think this pregnancy was planned."

"Agreed. And I hate the idea of her sleeping with someone who was also making her miserable—makes me want to cut off his nuts, the selfish prick."

Maybe, Pat thought, Julie couldn't bear that truth either and that was why she was so set on being with him. Was he just an eraser for her, someone to rewrite her last time with Lance? He wanted to be more than that, he wanted to believe they shared something personal, and that she wouldn't use him that way. But he just didn't know. He was in shock.

He rubbed his chest, where an ache had formed. He'd heard the saying that it was better to have loved and lost than never to have loved at all, but having suffered that loss, he wasn't sure that saying held true.

His entire life he secretly pined for her and dreamed of one day having her. He was finally starting to accept that he'd missed his chance, until the other night when he found everything he wanted, literally, sitting right in his lap.

Having Julie, even if only for a day, was the highlight of his life. It was the truest euphoria he'd ever known. But losing her… It would be a greater hell than anything he'd ever suffered.

His head hung low as a sense of defeat washed over him. He couldn't interfere with a family when children were involved. But what if Lance only got worse. What if his gaslighting and manipulation grew into physical abuse, abuse that reached the child?

Lance was a malignant narcissist, and Pat truly believed there was no changing him. Julie had read a few books, but maybe if he could convince her to speak to a professional, she would feel more confident in her choices.

He hadn't realized he'd reached for his phone, but as he stared down at it in his palm, a text message already open for Julie, he didn't have a clue what to write.

Shutting off the phone, he threw it on the bed. "Shit."

Jo rubbed a comforting hand down his back and rested her head on his shoulder. "If I'd known two days ago, I would have told you."

"I know." He just had to get through the next few hours and then he'd see her at the wedding. He'd know more once he saw her. He was never going to sleep tonight. "Want to crash here and binge *Schitt's Creek*?"

"Does the Pope shit in the woods?"

"Cool. I'll go raid the kitchen for snacks."

Jo passed out around one in the morning, and he stayed up, staring at the television but not really watching or listening to what was on the screen. Julie hadn't contacted him, and he wondered if she contacted Lance.

He thought about the fact that she was actually carrying another man's baby and outside of the family conflict, tried to determine if this at all affected his feelings for her. Around three in the morning, he decided it didn't.

He couldn't remember a time in his life, when he didn't love Julie. Even when he was a scrawny little boy, he'd do anything in his power to protect her. He loved the perfect way her hair curled at the tips and the imperfect way she snorted when she laughed. He didn't pick and choose the parts of her he loved. He loved all of her. And this child was a part of her.

Pat had always loved children and wanted a family. It was one of the reasons he wanted a financially stable career that let him set his own hours. Of course, he always pictured his life with Julie, even when it was clear she wasn't available. He tried not to think too deeply about their children. But his imagination had a mind of its own.

Sometimes he imagined they would have two girls and a boy. Other times he pictured a brood of wild Irish rogues and one delicate rose. It didn't matter how they were mixed. In the fantasy, they were always the same happy, loving family.

He realized he could handle raising another man's child. If it was a part of her, the other pieces didn't matter. But Julie was not in the same place as him.

For Julie to see this through and actually leave Lance for good, it couldn't be with Pat as plan B. She needed to do it on her own, like Jo said. And right now, Julie was scared.

Her confidence in herself was shaken after years of mental abuse and gaslighting. She might not believe she had it in her to raise a child right now, especially alone. But she would never truly be alone.

Pat knew she could do anything she put her mind to, but Julie needed to believe that. She needed to trust and believe in herself again. And that was what he wanted for her most of all.

He'd always be there to help with anything she needed, whether she loved him or not. That's what friendship was.

He hoped like hell she found the strength to stay away from Lance and move back home. If she stayed in Jasper Falls, he'd help her any way he could. And eventually, her confidence would return.

This was a big decision for her, one he couldn't rush her into. It now made sense why she kept saying that yesterday was an escape from reality, and she couldn't make any promises about what tomorrow would bring.

CHAPTER 15

"You look like you could use a swig." Perrin handed Pat a flask while they waited in the back room of O'Malley's for Ryan and Maggie to arrive after their last shoot with the photographer.

He sniffed the flask and scented whiskey, then took a swig and winced. "What the hell is this? Jameson?"

She snickered. "Your family has a weird loyalty to Tullamore Dew. Get over it." She sat beside him, the netting beneath the satin of her bridesmaid dress making a lot of noise at the simplest movement. "Don't mind me. I'm just a taffeta nightmare."

He glanced down at her feet and cocked his head. "Converse?"

"I have my limits."

He chuckled. Maggie and her sister weren't the girlie sort of girls. "You got a date out there?"

A cold laugh coughed out of her, and she took back her flask. "No, I don't date men."

"Women?" Maybe she'd like Jo.

"I wish. My life would be so much easier if women did it for me."

"Bad relationship?"

"You could say that. I'm surprised you didn't hear about it. Your cousin was screwed over by the same guy."

"I vaguely recall some gossip." He accepted the flask when she passed it back to him.

"How about you? Still pretending you're engaged to Jo Cook?"

He did a double take. "How did you—"

"I remember Jo from high school. I always assumed… Am I wrong?"

"No." His lips pressed in a rueful grin. "But if she did it for me life would be so easy."

"Funny how it works like that. Me, I'd rather be alone at this point. I can't deal with other people's bullshit anymore. I'll just take care of myself and know the job's done right."

He almost envied her, aside from part of him not fully believing what she said. Perrin was a beautiful woman. She was spunky and nice, and he couldn't help but see it as a loss to the world if she kept all that to herself.

"You never know," he said. "Sometimes life shocks the shit out of you and everything changes."

She studied him for a long moment. "Something shock the shit out of you recently?"

"You could say that."

They sat in a lengthy, comfortable silence, passing the flask back-and-forth until it was empty. The muffled voices from the front of the bar grew in volume as more guests began to arrive. The ceremony at the lake was beautiful, and he'd never seen his brother so happy. He needed to get out of his head and into the moment.

"What do you say I snag a bigger bottle from the front

and you and I do some pregaming while we wait for the bride and groom. I'll even get Tully."

Or he could get too drunk to think straight. "Deal."

~

Sweet Caroline BLASTED from the speakers as everyone waved linen napkins in the air and the DJ announced the parents of the bride and groom. O'Malley's was packed, the Irish relatives of the groom far outweighing the bride's family.

Julie smiled as Pat and Ryan's parents came out dancing with euphoric grins spread across their faces. Rosemarie looked to be having the time of her life. Maggie's parents were announced next and made a much more subdued entrance.

Next came the best man and maid of honor. Pat appeared with Perrin, the bride's sister, riding on his shoulders. His bowtie was loose, face rosy, after what she bet was several shots of whiskey, and he appeared to be having a ball.

Julie laughed, envious of their lighthearted mood and cheerful demeanor. She didn't know Perrin very well, but she seemed to fit right in with the Clooneys.

The music shifted to *The Blood of Cu Chulainn* and everyone stood as the DJ announced the bride and groom. Despite the high energy, her eyes watered. Time seemed to move in slow-motion as Ryan danced out of the back room, his beautiful wife smiling and twirling in his arms. The bride and groom's gazes glued to each other as all the heartaches of their pasts seemed to disappear.

Julie looked down at her hand, where her engagement ring usually rested. If she put the ring back on and married Lance, would their wedding be this happy? Would Lance ever look at her the way Ryan looked at Maggie?

The hair on the back of her neck lifted, and she turned to find Pat staring at her. He smiled and her heart fluttered. Would Lance ever look at her like *that*?

Chills raced over her shoulders as she tried to breathe evenly, but when he watched her with that penetrating stare, everything seemed to shake within her. She assumed by now Jo had told him. Yet he didn't seem angry with her.

The music changed again, cutting to the Beach Boys' *Don't Worry Baby,* and Ryan and Maggie shared their first official dance. Their happiness radiated across the room.

She'd been to many McCullough weddings, and this one wasn't any different. After the first dance, everyone flooded the dance floor and the meal began. Drinks poured, from an endless fountain, and by the main course, the majority of the guests were wasted.

After the dinner plates were cleared and the cake was cut, the chairs were mostly empty and the dance floor was full. Some of the older guests had taken their leave.

Pat hadn't approached her, and she supposed, that was best. He and Jo danced to a few quick songs, but he had been mostly preoccupied with his relatives.

Her phone buzzed from within her purse, and she stupidly checked the screen. No surprise it was Lance, calling her again. He'd been calling nonstop all day, even when he knew today was the wedding.

Before she could put the phone back in her purse, a text flashed on the screen. *I'm out front. Either meet me out here or I'm coming in.*

Her blood ran cold. Lance was there, all the way from Maryland?

She quickly stood, nearly knocking over a glass of chardonnay, and went to stop him from coming inside. Her gaze briefly crossed with Jo's on her way out the door, and she glimpsed her sister's concern but tried to wave it off, like she was just going out to get some air.

The evening humidity hit her like a brick wall. The music could be heard from the parking lot, but she didn't see Lance's car. Had she misunderstood? She checked her phone again.

"Where's your ring?"

Her spine stiffened and she turned, finding him lurking in the shadows. "What are you doing here, Lance?"

"I was invited."

"And you decided not to come. Lance, you have to go. I don't want to make a scene."

He pushed off the brick exterior and sauntered closer. He was wearing his good suit, the one he preferred for weddings. "They invited me, Julie. I have every right to be here. Ryan and I are old friends. You shouldn't have left without me."

She scoffed. "You said you weren't coming."

His eyes narrowed and he caught her chin in a tight pinch between his forefinger and thumb, angling her face upward and studying her. "You look different. Did you change your hair?"

She jerked her face away and took a step back. "I want you to leave."

"Why?" He looked at her left hand. "Why aren't you wearing your ring? You're always losing things. I shouldn't have gotten you such a nice piece of jewelry if you weren't going to take care of it."

"I took it off."

His sharp stare cut to her face, and her breath held in her lungs as he glared at her. "You're not supposed to do that," he said slowly. "When you put it on, you made a promise to me. I think it's time to come home."

She took another step back. "I'm not coming *home*." She

didn't know where she would live or where she would work, but she knew she didn't want to go back to Maryland.

"You've been here long enough. It's time to get back to reality, Julie."

"No. *This* is reality, Lance. I left. And I'm… I don't want to go back."

"What do you think this is?" he snapped. "You take off and get to come back when you feel like it? Your home is with me, in our house. It's time to come home. Get in the car."

She shook her head. "I don't want to live in Maryland anymore. I… I don't want to marry you."

His jaw ticked and his glare contorted. She braced for the expected stream of insults.

"You leave me and it's over, Julie. I've been carrying you for years, introducing you to friends, paying for your lifestyle, trying to show you how the better half lives. You think I need that sort of hassle? You never appreciated how much I've done for you, how much I had to convince others to give you a chance or invite you along, when the women were making plans. You're always lost in your head, bringing other people down or taking life too seriously. You never figured out how to have fun. You're lucky you're pretty, but you're getting older. What do you think will happen without me? You think you can do better?"

He laughed, the sound cold and chilling her to the bone, but he was far from finished. He wouldn't stop until he turned her into brittle ice and shattered her into a million pieces.

"Who's going to take care of you? Your family? You'll rot here. You'll never be happy in a town like this. You're spoiled, and without me that lifestyle you've grown so accustomed to will disappear. You don't have the brains to support yourself." He scoffed. "You can barely figure out what to make for dinner."

She refused to let him bate her, so she pressed her lips shut, but his words hit their mark and penetrated her steely exterior, slicing her heart to shreds. She kept her spine ramrod straight, letting him rail at her, taking it all in and reminding herself this was the real him.

A tear rolled down her cheek, and he paused from degrading her. His voice softened. "Come on, baby, let's not do this. I don't want to fight. Let's go home. We can take a few days to reconnect, like old times."

His polarized comments left her dizzy with a sense of whiplash. He reached for her hand, and she jerked back. "Don't touch me."

His gentle expression hardened. "I'll tell everyone the things you said about them."

She hadn't said anything negative about anyone. It was Lance who always complained and talked behind their friends' backs. She rarely interrupted or disagreed, so in his head, he probably thought she felt the same way. And he'd said terrible things about them. She'd lose all of them, and they'd think she was an awful person.

He'd set himself up for just such an escape, always insisting on extreme privacy, wanting to live far away from her family and friends in Pennsylvania, and threading embarrassing truths through every stitch of turmoil, so she wouldn't bother explaining how bad things had gotten along the way.

He always, even at his worst, made sure she felt somewhat culpable. It's how he kept her quiet and ashamed for so long, fearful others would judge her. And in Maryland, she had no one who would believe her word against his, because he'd arranged it that way. He was always so doting when others were watching, a master performer who took method acting to the extreme.

"I mean it, Julie, you either get your ass in that car and come home, or we're finished. I won't let you come back."

Her body began to shake, and she wanted to scream. He meant it. She had no doubt Lance would move on, just to spite her. He'd make sure she somehow saw him moving on, too. Despite the horrible things he said and the unbalanced way he made her feel, part of her still loved him, and seeing him with someone else would hurt.

That was the ugly truth of abuse. And that was the moment she truly recognized herself as a victim. But, more importantly, that was the moment she decided she wasn't going to be a victim anymore. It was a choice—*her* choice—and she had finally made up her mind to get away from him, no matter the consequence.

Her bones seemed to tremble as she held his stare. "I can't be with you anymore, Lance. I need to be myself, and I can be that when I'm with you."

"It's always about you, isn't it? This is just more of the same old drama. You're never satisfied with the way things are. Good luck getting your shit back. I'm throwing it away as soon as I get home. I should have listened to everyone else and not wasted my time with you. You disgust me!"

With that, he stormed off into the dark lot and peeled away. For a moment, she feared he might try to run her over, but then he was gone.

She exhaled the moment the taillights disappeared, her hands shaking violently. The sound of gravel scraping underfoot startled her, and she looked up to find Jo and Pat approaching. She burst into tears, knowing they heard the entire thing.

Jo was there, hugging her and telling her she'd be all right. But Pat stood back, cautiously watching her. She couldn't stop sobbing and was certain there would be no returning to the wedding.

"I should have slashed his tires, but then we never would've gotten rid of him," Jo said.

"What am I going to do?" What if she couldn't do this on her own? She had no job, no money, no place to live, and a baby on the way. She'd have to, eventually, contact him again to tell him about the baby. He'd have rights, and she'd be tied to him for the rest of her life through their child. She didn't know if she had the strength to handle that.

"You're going to cry and then you're going to clean yourself up and do whatever you have to do, Jules. You're strong and capable, and you'll get through this."

A jagged breath shook her as she looked over her sister's shoulder to find Pat's watchful stare on her. His eyes were tense with concern, and she could only imagine what he thought of her after hearing all the terrible things Lance said.

Jo took a step back. "I should go back inside, give you two a chance to talk." With one last squeeze to Julie's hand, she let go and headed back to the bar, affectionately tapping Pat's shoulder on the way.

They stood in silence, several feet apart.

"I can imagine what you think of me—"

"No, you can't."

His abrupt interruption stunted any excuses she'd planned to make. She couldn't read his expression enough to tell if he was angry or upset or disgusted.

"I just watched a man try to tear you down with every insult he could think of and you didn't flinch. You didn't see what I saw. You didn't see the woman I love raise her chin and face down her tormentor. You didn't watch her tremble. You didn't feel me shaking with her. You don't know the rage that burned through me at hearing someone speak to you that way. It probably scarred me for life. And you don't know how hard it was for me to let you handle that on your own. So, let's not pretend you know what I'm thinking."

Her head lowered and humiliation knifed through her. She never wanted him to witness this side of her life. She brought this ugliness here, and now, he'd never forget it.

"When I saw that tear roll down your face, I wanted to slaughter him," Pat rasped. "But then I realized what you were doing. You lived with him. You know how a toxic narcissist's thinking works. There's no arguing with their alternate reality. They make it whatever suits them at the time. He couldn't handle your rejection, so he needed to turn it into his."

Her head lifted and she nodded. "The books say a break up with a narcissist has to be sudden and is almost always brutal."

He closed the distance and didn't stop until he was holding her face. "I hate that he hurt you."

"Me, too." Another tear fell and he kissed it away. "I hate that you heard the things he said."

"None of it's true, Julie. He has no idea who you really are. He's only ever cared about himself." His lips found hers, and he kissed her again and again, as though he needed the reassurance of knowing he could.

"I have to tell you…"

"I already know about the baby."

Her breath caught as the fear of losing him left her staggered. Over the past forty-eight hours, she accepted that Lance would always be a part of her past and her future would never be certain. There was so little people could actually control in life, but she knew she wanted a future with Patrick, if he'd have her.

She wiped her eyes, a smear of makeup coming away with her spent tears. "Are you mad?"

He looked at her, his eyes a tumultuous storm of emotion she couldn't decipher. "This baby's a part of you."

A shaky smile trembled to her lips as she understood he'd

already accepted the situation. No matter what her future held, she was keeping the baby.

"Life's always gonna have surprises, Jules. Every relationship faces complications. The good ones belong to the couples that figure out how to work through those challenges together. If you let me help you, I'd be honored. But I also know you're strong enough to handle this or any obstacle on your own."

She looked up at him with glassy eyes, her words wedged tightly in her throat. He'd known for less than a day, but he'd worked it all out and come to terms with it, no backlash or put-downs necessary. Was this what a healthy relationship felt like?

"I love you, Pat."

How could she not? He was the most understanding person she'd ever met. She was beyond lucky for having found him again.

"You're the *best* man I know."

He kissed her and the chill in her bones thawed. She laughed against his lips, in awe that this was where they were and everything might, for once, turn out okay. Then the door opened.

"Julie?"

Pat broke the kiss and they turned, finding her mother and father gaping at them. "Mom."

"What are you doing? Where's Josephine?" She turned her disapproving scowl on Pat. "How dare you!"

"Mom, wait, you don't understand."

"You're engaged to someone else, and he's engaged to your sister! What could I possibly be missing?"

"You don't know the whole story—"

"I'm not engaged to Jo. We're just friends," Pat burst. "She didn't want you to fix her up, so she pretended we were engaged."

Her mother scoffed, her denial quickly morphing to fury. "She's shameless!"

Pat was through with the lies and wanted everything out in the open. "I'm in love with your daughter, Julie."

Her mother looked to be having some sort of episode, clearly appalled by such a scandal. "You're too late."

"No, Mom. Lance and I are through."

Her mother's face paled. "Through? You promised to marry him. There is no *through.* You've already lived under his roof, in his bed... In God's eyes, you're as good as married."

"I'm sorry you see it that way. But I've made up my mind."

Pat's hand closed over hers and squeezed tightly. She felt his support as she stood her ground.

The door opened again, and Jo rushed out. She looked like she'd been hoping to intercept but was a minute too late. "Oh, good, you're all here." She looked at her sister and Pat and made an apologetic shrug.

"You lied to me in my own home," their mother sneered, turning her scorn on Jo. "What did I ever do to raise such a hateful—"

"That's it!" Jo snapped. "What have I ever done that was so hateful other than try to be myself? It's *you* who hates me, Mom. You take issue with everything I do, from the way I dress and wear my hair, to the way I run my life. It's no wonder I moved away. My life is peaceful in Philly. I don't have to constantly worry about what others might think. As a matter of fact, I don't give a shit what anyone thinks anymore. I thought I did. That's why I made Pat lie for me. But you know what? It's too hard pretending to be someone I'm not."

Julie let go of Pat's hand and moved to her sister's side, then laced her fingers with hers. Pat followed, taking Jo's other hand, forming a wall of support around her.

Jo looked at her parents and said, "I'm gay. I like women. So, please stop trying to fix me up with your friends' sons, and please start accepting me for who I am."

"Oh! You're just hateful!" their mother screamed, releasing a diatribe of insults and painful truths neither Julie nor Jo were prepared to hear.

It was the first time Julie saw her sister flinch. Each awful insult screamed from their mother's mouth pelted them like buckshot, leaving all of them injured in the end.

It was no secret that their mother hadn't wanted children but felt obligated as a wife. She'd wished for sons, but was cursed with twin girls in the middle. In all of her screaming and tears, she actually used the word *cursed* and something in Julie clicked.

No matter how broken her life seemed or how scared she was, her circumstances were not cursed. Her hand pressed protectively to her stomach, as if to protect her child.

It was the first time she felt trust in herself again. It didn't matter how awful her baby's father might have been, she trusted herself to be a caring and loving mother. She knew, without a doubt, that she would accept her baby no matter what and always be there for him or her, the way a good mother should.

When her father finally dragged their mom away, her hysterics spiraling into prayers and tears, Julie realized something she never wanted to see. Her mother and Lance were alike in a lot of ways, only Lance justified his behavior through social status, where her mother rooted her self-righteousness in religion. In the end, they were both hiding a lifetime of insecurities behind a mask made of their own self-absorption so others wouldn't hold them accountable for lacking such natural traits as empathy and acceptance.

"Are you okay?" Pat asked Jo once their parents were gone.

Jo had always been the resilient one, but there was no hiding how much her mother's scorn and rejection had wounded her.

"I'll live." When her words came out raw, she cleared her throat. "I always expected it would go something like that."

Julie looked at her, wishing she could somehow take away her pain. "I love you, Jo. I just want you to be happy. Mom's wrong. And I think her beliefs are wrong, if that means anything at all to you."

"It does." She smiled, but there was pain masked in her eyes. Pacing away, she let out a hard breath. "I'm gonna head back to the city tonight."

"Stay," Pat insisted. "You can crash at my parents'."

"No. I think I'd be a bit of a third wheel there. It's cool. I miss my own bed anyway."

They tried to persuade her to stay, but it was no use. Sometimes people just needed time to process agony in private, so they could put it away and make room to be happy again. It wasn't something anyone could rush.

Julie gave her a hug, not wanting to let her go yet. "Promise you'll text when you get there. And let's not go so long without seeing each other again. I can come to the city if that's easier."

Jo nodded. "So, you're staying in Jasper Falls?"

Julie shrugged and blushed. "They're getting a hot doctor here."

"Gross." But Jo laughed. Holding her arms out to Pat, she made her goodbyes, and they watched her drive away.

Pat's hand curved around Julie's naturally, as though he'd been holding it forever, and she leaned into his strength. "Do you want to go back inside?"

"No, but I have to."

She checked her phone. "There's only about an hour left.

Go enjoy the rest of your brother's wedding. I'll follow in a second."

"You're coming back in?"

She nodded. "I missed you too much to let another second pass me by."

He bent his head and kissed her. "I love you."

"And I feel it. Do you feel me loving you back?"

"I've always felt it, Jules. That's why I've never been able to resist you. You're the easiest person in the world to love."

He kissed her again, and she begrudgingly nudged him toward the party. "Go, or you'll miss the end of the receptions. I'll be right behind you."

"Fine, but as soon as this is over, it's on. I'm telling everyone the truth first thing in the morning. No more lies. No more hiding."

"Um, duh. But I can't wait until morning. I was planning on sneaking in your window tonight."

"I'll leave it open. But as of tomorrow morning, we're using the front door. I've always said one day you'd be mine. That day's tomorrow."

"And after that?"

He smiled. "After that, we start the rest of our life together."

With one last promising glance over his shoulder, he disappeared into the bar.

Julie reached into her purse and fished out her engagement ring. The glittering diamond reminded her of an anchor more than any sort of uplifting gem. Without hesitation, she dropped it in the parking lot and walked inside, taking her first steps toward a brighter future.

EPILOGUE

"You're all set, Mr. McGinty. Here's your lab script, and Dr. Clooney will see you in two months."

"Thank you, sweetheart."

Julie smiled as little old Mr. McGinty fixed his hat and pushed out the door. She shut off her computer and stacked the files from the day. On her way through the waiting room, she locked the front door and lowered the curtain.

"I don't like when he calls you sweetheart. Especially when he came this close to marrying you in a game of *Fuck, Marry, Kill,*" Pat said as he leaned against the doorway watching her.

He'd removed his lab coat, and the sleeves of his dress shirt were rolled up to the elbows. She reached for a canister of cleaning wipes and began sanitizing the waiting room chairs, making sure he had a decent view of her backside every time she bent down.

"Yes…" he groaned. "Disinfect those dirty chairs."

She giggled, squatting low in her dress to straighten the magazines. "Whatever does it for you."

"You do it for me."

She rolled her eyes and shut off the television. Emptying the trash can, she carried the bag to the back and washed her hands.

"Don't forget, tomorrow Mrs. Westby is coming in for her physical. She likes to get here early, so make sure you're here at eight on the dot."

"Yes, ma'am."

"And your Aunt Col wants you to look at a mole on her back."

"Did she make an appointment?"

She gave him a skeptical glance. "Your aunts never make appointments."

"You have to tell them that's how this works."

"I've tried. They just say they'll swing by when they can."

"You let them get away with that because they bring you cookies."

She turned and rested a hand on her protruding belly. "Are you implying something about my weight?"

Her ring glinted against the fabric, and he closed the distance, resting a hand directly over hers. "Only that I love the shape of you."

"Good." She kissed his nose. "Tonight, I'm craving extra spicy Thai and a mint chocolate chip shake."

"Two steps ahead of you. I bought mint chocolate chip ice cream yesterday at the store."

She flipped off the light. "That's why I love you."

Together they walked up the stairs to their apartment and stripped out of their work clothes. He followed her into the shower and took his time covering her body in suds and kisses.

"How are you feeling today?"

She'd been having some early contractions that morning. "Better. I think it'll be soon."

"Sheilagh said to give her a call as soon as you're ready to start your leave. She's ready to cover for you." His touch turned clinical, and she rolled her eyes.

"I prefer when you don't examine me in the shower, Dr. Clooney."

"Just checking."

"You know, sex is supposed to speed things along." She struggled to see how anyone could find her attractive in this state, but Pat seemed to have no problem there.

He shut off the water and handed her a towel. "Careful." Taking her arm so she didn't slip, he led her to the bedroom. "Now, let's see if we can speed this along."

They made love and she saw no point in getting dressed. When the Thai food arrived, Pat brought it to her in bed. They ate and talked about their day, then he made her the perfect milkshake for dessert.

Cocooned in his arms and a sense of peace, she reveled in a safe feeling of happiness. Her new life seemed pretty perfect.

She was just drifting to sleep when a sharp kick woke her and she sucked in an audible breath.

Pat met her stare with a look of concern. "Did you feel something?"

She massaged her side and frowned. "I'm not sure if it's the Thai or a contract—*ah!* Definitely a contraction."

He checked the time, and forty minutes later they were calling the midwife. Pat had prepared for this moment. He had one of the patient rooms arranged with perinatal equipment, calming music, but he, himself, had way too much excitement to watch her pass a human through her most tender parts.

Thank goodness for his training and natural calm, because once those contractions formed a pattern, she was a hot, screaming mess. The midwife was cool and collected, focused completely on her comfort, which there wasn't much of. After several hours of laborious breathing and pushing, their daughter had finally arrived.

She was beautiful, with a swirl of golden hair and a perfect little nose. Julie cradled her in her arms and shivered, her hair damp with sweat and her eyes full of tears.

"You were amazing," Pat whispered, staring down at Julie and touching the baby's tiny fingers. "She's gorgeous, like her mother."

She looked up at him and smiled. "She's ours."

She'd waited until her second trimester to tell Lance about the pregnancy. By that time, he'd already moved on and was dating someone else. Lance showed little interest in the baby, and Pat had researched the adoption process. The papers were prepared and Pat planned to have them sent to Lance this morning. By the time they signed the birth certificate, her daughter would be fully theirs.

"Do you have a name?" the midwife asked.

"Fiona Clooney," she said, smiling. She'd be a Clooney before Julie, but that was fine. In two months, Julie would become Mrs. Patrick Clooney for the rest of her life.

Part of her wondered if that was always who she was intended to be. Pat believed it was. He said he saw their life a million different ways in his dreams, imagined their future every night before he went to sleep.

She no longer questioned her sanity or worried something might be lacking in her logic. The moment she found stable ground, her life settled and she saw things more clearly.

Pat was a steady presence in her heart, always so loving, supportive, and accepting. She felt honored to have him as her partner, and when she did little things to show him how much he meant to her, he always noticed and appreciated the gesture.

She realized life didn't have to be intense for it to be

happy. Love didn't have to be volatile to be passionate. And being with someone else should never mean leaving parts of yourself behind.

"Am I too late?"

Julie lifted her stare and smiled at Jo's frazzled entrance. "Just in time."

"Oh, my God." Her sister threw her bags on the empty seat and crossed the room. "It's a girl?"

Julie nodded. "Fiona."

"Oh, Jules, she's perfect." She turned her glittering eyes up at Pat. "Isn't she perfect?"

"Perfect." He nodded. "And, just like it was with her mom —love at first sight."

THE END

Keep scrolling for a sneak peek into the next Jasper Falls novel, LOVE ME NOTS

And don't forget to claim your FREE gift, a copy of ALMOST PRIEST (McCullough Mountain 1)

FREE GIFT & MORE JASPER FALLS!

START READING THE NEXT BOOK IN THE JASPER FALLS SERIES

Keep scrolling to enjoy a sneak peek into
LOVE ME NOTS (Jasper Falls 3)
Available June 2021!

****

Claim Your Gift!
Book 1 of the McCullough Mountain Series is FREE!
Download ALMOST PRIEST Now!
This 8 book, small-town, BIG family romance takes you back to the beginning!

OTHER BOOKS BY LYDIA MICHAELS

Love Me Nots

La Vie en Rose

"Heart Wrenchingly Beautiful!"

Breaking Perfect

"Delicious and Dirty!"

Blind (FREE)

Untied

First Comes Love (FREE)

If I Fall

Something Borrowed

Protégé

"Secret Kink Society!"

Simple Man

"Unexpected Baby/Fatherhood"

The Surrender Trilogy

"Drama, Betrayal, Scandal, Oh my!"

The McCullough Mountain Series

(Book #1 FREE)

The Degrees of Separation Trilogy

(Book #1 FREE)

The Calamity Rayne Series

(Book #1 FREE!)

Hurt

"Hauntingly Dark Romance! A Masterpiece!"

LOVE ME NOTS

"Hey, Perrin, I've been waitin' on that beer for over—"

Perrin cracked open a bottle of bud and slid it across the counter to Mac, one of the more restless locals. "I know," she said patiently, eyes on her regular while mixing a pitcher of sugar-free mojitos for the group of female tourists that just sauntered in. "Cut me a little slack. Singles Week is kicking my ass."

Jasper Falls used to be just an average, nameless, small town lost in the middle of Center County. Since the new mayor got elected, the town's been really revamping itself.

Singles Week was just one of the new events Jasper Falls was running—part of the town's revitalization project. It was great for local business owners like herself, but small-town folk generally preferred to move at a slower pace, which tourists did not, especially the New York ones.

"Sorry, sweetie." Mac plugged up his mouth with his beer and leered at the group of long-legged blondes. "Women certainly didn't look like that when I was shoppin' for a wife."

Perrin tsked and shot him a disapproving look. "Stop that. Nadine's a catch."

"Yeah," he chuckled. "The kind you throw back."

Topping off the pitcher with a shot of simple syrup and another handful of fresh mint from the farmers' market, she shook her head. "You're rotten. Someone should throw *you* back."

"Hey," he called, just as she lifted the tray of mojitos and glasses. "How come you ain't signed up for those singles events?"

Perrin's lips pressed in a tight-lipped purse as she shot him a sidelong glance. "You know perfectly well why. I don't date."

He shook his head and sipped his beer. "You're wastin' your youth, missy."

"Better to waste my youth than to waste my time." Before he could offer another unwanted comment, she carried the tray over to the blondes.

O'Malley's was packed with the typical Friday night crowd. Each weekend the crowd increased, which was great for business, however not so great for Perrin's poor aching feet. It was long past the time to hire another waitress, but Perrin didn't want to spare the expense, despite what her sister Maggie had to say about it.

"Here you go, ladies. Can I get you anything else?"

She pulled a notepad out of her apron pocket when one woman asked, "Are your salads farm to table?"

Perrin grit her molars and grinned. "Actually, all our produce is locally farmed." Thank goodness for Ashlynn and her farmers' market. The more New Yorkers they got, the more she was getting these sorts of questions. Next would be the bread.

"It says your salad comes with a dinner roll. Is it gluten-free?"

"We have handcrafted breads with an almond flour option," thanks to Maggie's amazing mother-in-law.

Once Perrin answered several more questions about the menu and if the lettuce could be substituted with kale, she finally had an order together. Sue was going to kill her.

She walked the order to the kitchen, catching six more drink orders on the way. "Sue, I need some salads." Sticking the slip on the order rack, she quickly slipped out the back.

"What the fuck, Perrin!" Sue bolted out of the kitchen. "These aren't on the menu"

Perrin smiled and uncapped two light beers. "Everything's on the menu. We're adapting."

"Well, we need an actual cook! And do we even have kale?"

Luckily, she just bought some that morning. "In the back. Check the bottom crisper."

She returned to the kitchen grumbling something about bullshit hipsters and their high maintenance diets. Sue was O'Malley's senior bartender—came with the purchase of the bar, sort of like the dusty old pool tables and vinyl stools, when they bought the place last year. She was great at bartending, passable at cooking, but best as a waitress. Unfortunately, they were understaffed in all three areas, so Sue was a constant fill in.

"Here you are, boys." Perrin dropped the two beers off at a high-top and worked her way through the crowd, zigzagging between the bar and tables for the next few hours.

By the end of the night, she'd have well over twenty-five thousand steps on her pedometer, blisters on her toes, and sweat stains on her clothes, but it was worth it. She finally got her sister to agree to expand the bar—*if* Perrin could figure out a way to scrape together the down payment.

The land behind the bar had been listed for about six months. They needed twenty thousand down, if they wanted to get approved for financing. They had the bar as collateral and, luckily, the bank still loved supporting local merchants. She was crossing her fingers that was enough to get them approved, even when they were offering sixty thousand less than the asking price. Perrin was pretty sure she'd do anything short of giving up *both* her kidneys to own the property.

Lots of *ifs*. But buying O'Malley's with Maggie had been one of the greatest investment risks of her life, and it's been paying off ever since. Jasper Falls was rising as one of Pennsylvania's greatest small towns. O'Malley's used to be the *only* night spot—just the average hole-in-the-wall Irish pub, but now, with all the revitalization projects and new restaurants cropping up, they had some competition.

O'Malley's needed to rebrand and get with the times, cater to the younger crowd. Perrin was all over that—in a sort of trash to treasure way. She'd been researching affordable ideas to hit that earthy hot spot vibe that was trending.

"Yo, Perrin!"

Before she could turn, her body was hoisted into the air and the bar spun. "Put me down!" Then the bear-hug came, and she recognized the giant arms squeezed around her waist. "Luke."

He dropped her back to her feet and gave an unabashed grin. "Hey, beautiful. How's it going?"

"Busy. Can't you tell?"

He followed her back to the bar. "Busy's good. No Ryan tonight?"

"No. He and Maggie are having a *date night*." She used air quotes to show her disregard for such rituals. Ryan and Maggie were married. Wasn't every encounter a date?

She slid Luke a beer, and he took a long sip, eyeing her with plenty of palpable judgement. "Bitter's a bad color on you."

"Who says I'm bitter?" She was. It wasn't a secret. But she liked to know who was talking crap, so she could mind her six.

Luke chuckled, deciding not to respond and eyed the crowd. The band had started to play, which meant more people dancing and less drink orders for a few minutes. "You need a hand?"

"It's calm right now. But if it picks back up…" She leaned on the bar, taking some of the weight off her tired feet. "Where's Tristan?"

"He's helping Alexia with her school project. She has to build a diorama, and apparently, to my husband, that means power tools and upcycling anything we're not using around the house."

She smiled, because they were possibly the cutest blended family in the world. Luke wasn't Alexia's biological father, but Tristan, Luke's husband, had stepped up when Luke's brother-in-law, Alec, had been unable to get Sheilagh pregnant. So although Luke didn't share Tristan's biological link to Alexia, he still treated her as his own, so Alexia technically had three fathers who spoiled her rotten—Luke, Tristan, and Alec. Poor girl was going to have a hell of a time dating when the time came.

The door opened, drawing her attention, as a tall man with a head of black hair stepped in. Another New Yorker. She could always tell by the clothes and polished appearance of their skin. The locals tended to favor denim, cotton, and flannel. They also had skin that seemed slightly…weathered. More sun, less makeup, and plenty of freckles from outdoor work.

Luke studied the man as he sat down at the bar. She shot him a look and hid a smirk, silently agreeing that the newcomer was worth looking at.

Despite his overly GQ clothing, his dark eyes hid something rugged. Something that drew a girl in as much as it warned her to stay away. He slid a black card across the bar.

"I'll take a glass of Glenfiddich, please."

Wow. That voice cut through her like a knife through butter on a hot day. She shook her head and cleared her throat. "Glen what?"

His full lips curved into a half smile. "Glenfiddich. It's Scotch."

"Oh." She placed an O'Malley's coaster in front of him. "Sorry. We don't carry that. And we don't accept this." She pushed his card back. "Can I get you a standard whiskey? We have Jameson and Tully. Or if you prefer Scotch, we have Dewar's."

He nodded without any show of irritation. "Dewar's. Neat."

She poured the drink, and when she turned back around, a fifty rested on the bar. She quickly changed it out.

Luke eyed the newcomer. "You coming in from New York?"

"Houston."

His brows shot up in surprise. They didn't usually get visitors from that far south.

"My husband's from Texas," Luke said, eyeing the man for any unwanted reaction. It was well-known that Luke and Tristan had faced their fair share of harassment back in the day.

The locals had done a good job of chasing the bigots out of Jasper Falls, but with so many newcomers, one never knew who they were dealing with. The world was a crazy, sometimes hateful, place.

Surprise flashed in the man's dark eyes, but he made no other physical response. "Which part?"

"A little backwoods town called Luckenbach."

"Yeah, I know where that is. Just outside of Fredericksburg, right?"

"Right." Luke put down his beer and held out a hand. "Luke McCullough."

"Gage King."

Perrin drew in a breath, and the testosterone coming off the two of them nearly choked her.

"This here is Perrin. She owns the bar."

Gage tipped his head in a casual nod. "Perrin."

"Hi." She couldn't quite work out a bigger greeting, because her brain seemed to have disintegrated into ash the moment he locked eyes with her. As the corners of his mouth curved upward, her ovaries exploded. "I gotta go check a…thing."

Shooting a thumb over her shoulder, she escaped to the kitchen. Sue was rummaging through the back freezer, cursing as she jostled several filled bins.

"Sue," Perrin hissed, her gaze peeking through the order window at Luke and Gage.

"What?" she snapped.

Perrin frowned at her tone but only glanced over her shoulder and then back to the men. She only had a few seconds before someone needed a refill. "There's a hot guy at the bar."

Sue was suddenly beside her. "Well, *hello* handsome. Who is he?"

"He's from Houston."

She frowned. "What's he doing all the way up here?"

Perrin shrugged. "I don't know, but he's not wearing a ring."

Sue's brows shot up. "You noticed that?"

"I…I guess I did."

"Then you should ask him out."

Now it was Perrin's turn to frown. "Get real. You know I don't date."

"Girl, you have got to get over your shit." She tipped her head toward the bar. "I bet getting under that hunk of man out there would get you over it really quick."

When she walked away, Perrin did a double take. "Aren't you interested?"

"Nope." She disappeared back into the freezer.

"Why not?"

"Because finders keepers. You saw him first."

"I'm not interested." Three customers stepped up to the bar at once, expressions going from searching to impatient in two seconds flat. "You're wasting a perfect piece of man candy."

"Then you better step in."

Rolling her eyes, she went to help the customers. For the next hour, she barely had time to think. As the rush slowed, the bar was less full and the tables were starting to thin. Luke still sat at the bar, but he and the man no longer spoke. They seemed content to simply stare at the flat screens and watch some sports show Luke had put on. Since the bar used to belong to his family, he often helped himself to the remote.

"Refill?" she asked.

Luke waved her off, but Gage slid his empty glass forward. "How long have you owned the bar?"

"A little over a year."

"How's business? Is this an ordinary crowd?"

She refilled his Scotch. "Actually, this is a little busier than the norm, but each weekend seems to generate a bigger crowd than the last—especially since the revitalization project started."

He nodded his approval. "So business is good? Steady?"

Business was great. "I can't complain. What do you do?"

"Ever hear of King's Construction Outlet?"

Luke turned, his eyes narrowing and his ears practically perking.

"Yeah, I've seen their commercials." Everyone had. They were the country's leading hardware and lumber distributor. Pop-up box stores were in every town, but Jasper Falls did their best to avoid the larger chain companies in favor of mom-and-pop stores.

"I'm Gage King," he said as if that explained everything.

Perrin's eyes widened. "Like King as in *King*?"

He chuckled. "Correct."

"As in you're *the* King."

He chuckled again. "That's one way of looking at it." He reached in the breast pocket of his suit jacket and pulled out a business card, sliding it across the bar.

It didn't have the orange logo of King's Construction on it, and it wasn't a normal paper business card. This one was thick like a credit card and pearl white. It only said Gage King on the front. The back had a phone number and email.

"That's my personal card."

Luke's gaze narrowed. "You hear on business or pleasure?"

"A little of both."

Oh boy. That wasn't going to go over well. Everyone knew Jasper Falls was most famous for its lumber. McCullough Lumber was owned by three generations of McCullough men. *Everyone* worked there, including her brother-in-law, Ryan, who also happened to be a co-owner with Luke and his twin brother Finn.

"What kind of business?" Luke all but growled. Gone was the friendly bar patron attitude from earlier.

"Just keeping my options open."

And apparently, keeping his plans to himself. Perrin shot Luke a look, warning him to play nice. This guy was still a paying customer.

Luke tossed some cash on the bar and grabbed his jacket. "I'll see you later, Perrin."

"Bye, Luke." She sighed. Within ten minutes, every McCullough in a ten mile radius was going to be gossiping about this guy. And there were *a lot* of McCulloughs.

"Something I said?" Gage asked, glancing over his shoulder as Luke left the bar.

"His family owns the lumberyard up on the mountain."

"Ah." He sipped his Scotch.

Since he didn't offer any further information about his intentions, Perrin did her own digging. "So, are you really thinking about putting one of your stores here?"

He eyed her skeptically. "Do you have an opinion on the matter?"

"I've got lots. But it's rude to answer a question with a question."

He chuckled. "I'm undecided. I could be convinced either way. How about we have dinner and you do your best to persuade me?"

She frowned. "You don't know which way I'll try to sway you."

He glanced at Luke's empty seat and arched a brow, as if somehow challenging her. Crossing his arms on the bar, he leaned forward. "If I hesitated every time I came across a family-owned business, I'd barely own a single store."

She crossed her arms over her chest, pursing her lips. "And how many do you own?"

"Thirteen hundred."

The number literally knocked her back a step. She blinked, unable to mentally calculate such a vast collection of stores. "So," she said with a touch of sarcasm, "this is really a life-and-death endeavor for you."

He smirked. "You don't approve."

"You have *thirteen hundred* stores. Luke's my friend.

McCullough Lumber is family owned, and it employs half the residents of Jasper Falls. My brother-in-law and his cousin own it, minus their parents' shares. My customers rely on it. Can you offer jobs to everyone you'd be putting out of work?"

"We outsource our lumber."

"Locally?"

"Not always. But there are exceptions to every rule."

Her eyes narrowed. "I don't buy it. I think you big-box stores care more about your bottom-line than you do the people you put out of work or the habitats you hurt. I'm willing to bet you get tons of wood from rain forests."

"A ton is a rather small measurement in construction."

"You know what I mean."

"You seem very passionate about wood."

She wasn't. She just didn't want to see half the town unemployed, because some fancy suit showed up and changed everything. Plus, she had a lot of pent up aggression and no outlet, since she gave up sex more than a year ago.

Gage sighed and sat back, his broad shoulders and body language sending all sorts of haywire messages to her baby maker. "Less than four percent of our lumber comes from the Amazon. The majority of our supply comes from companies in North America. I can't give your friend any guarantees, but I'm always open to negotiation with any interested suppliers—big or small."

Well, that was something. "Okay then."

"Okay?"

"Okay." She uncrossed her arms.

He smiled, his dark eyes creasing at the corners. "Do you work tomorrow?"

"I work every day. It's the perk of being an owner." She wasn't complaining. Owning the bar was a blast, and she loved her independence.

"I thought you had a partner."

"I do. My sister, Maggie. But she handles the other stuff. I'm the onstage talent." She flashed him a cheeky grin and tossed out some jazz hands.

The creases at his eyes deepened. "When do you have off?"

A siren screamed in her head. She hadn't meant to flirt. It was sort of a natural response to being so close to a modern-day piece of Sparta perfection. But now that she realized what she'd been doing, her guard went up. "Why?"

"I'd like to take you to dinner."

Mayday, mayday, mayday! She took a step back, her butt hitting the counter behind her. "Sorry, I don't date."

His gaze dropped to her hand. "Married?"

"No."

His head cocked. "Gay?"

She wished. "No."

He frowned. "Am I missing something?"

"No. I just don't date."

"Ever?"

She shrugged. "It's been a while."

He studied her for a long minute, then finished his drink and stood. "We'll work on that." He pushed the change from his fifty across the bar to the gutter. "See you around, Perrin."

Nervous and confused, she said, "See ya."

How long was he planning on staying in Jasper Falls? And what were they going to work on?

After closing, she cleaned the bar and had a drink with Sue, retelling the whole Gage conversation. She was blown away by the possibility of a King's Construction Outlet opening in the town, but that wasn't what was most concerning at the moment to her.

"What do you think he meant by saying we'll work on that?"

Sue stood and gathered her empty bottle. "Oh, that just means he plans on banging you."

Perrin spit a sip of beer across the table. "What?"

"Come on, Perrin. Don't play dense. You two had chemistry. He's hot. Go for it."

She wiped off the table and followed Sue into the back, where the staff kept their coats and purses. "He can plan all he wants. I'm celibate."

Sue stuffed her arms into her coat. "And whose fault is that?"

It was hers, but it was totally a choice. Ever since she caught her fiancé cheating, sex had lost its appeal. Too many doubts and trust issues.

Still, she couldn't help imagining sex with Gage, just for a moment, in the safety of her own head. He probably had a killer body under that suit. And his hands looked big and strong. Masculine hands. He didn't have the hands of a man who worked at a desk, despite his professional attire.

She bet he was big in other areas too. He probably—

Realizing where her thoughts were leading, she shook her head. "I can't bang the guy threatening to put the town out of work."

Sue laughed and slung her purse over her shoulder. "But you thought about it for a second."

"No, I didn't."

"Liar." She opened the back door and glanced over her shoulder. "It's just dinner, Perrin. Baby steps. Every man isn't Bran. Let someone take you out and see how it goes. Do it for yourself, not for him."

Lips pressed into a flat line, she tried to bring herself to agree but couldn't promise anything. The thought of doing anything even slightly vulnerable made her queasy. "Drive safe."

She watched Sue walk to her car, then locked up. As she

walked to the back hall, she shut off the bar lights. Unlocking the door to her loft apartment, she glanced back at the dim bar and smiled.

This was hers. She didn't need a man. She had everything she needed right here.

ABOUT THE AUTHOR

Lydia Michaels is the author of over thirty-five novels and the consecutive winner of the 2018 & 2019 ***Author of the Year Award*** from ***Happenings Media,*** as well as the recipient of the 2014 ***Best Author Award*** from the ***Courier Times***. She has been featured in ***USA Today, Romantic Times Magazine, Love & Lace,*** and more. As the host and founder of the ***East Coast Author Convention***, the ***Behind the Keys Author Retreat,*** and ***Read Between the Wines,*** she continues to celebrate her growing love for readers and romance novels around the world.

Lydia is happily married to her childhood sweetheart. Some of her favorite things include the scent of paperback books, listening to her husband play piano, escaping to her coastal home at the Jersey Shore, cheap wine, 80's pop culture, coffee, and kilts. She hopes to meet you soon at one of her many upcoming events. You can follow Lydia at www.Facebook.com/LydiaMichaels

ACKNOWLEDGEMENT

This book and so many others would not be complete without the insight of my devoted editor, Theresa Kohler, whom I thank for all of her incredible work and attention to detail. Every Jasper Falls book also shines because of the amazing beta team behind the scenes. Lauren, Perrin, and Loren, I adore you! Thank you so much for all your feedback and great input!

Xo,
Lydia

Lightning Source UK Ltd.
Milton Keynes UK
UKHW040725270421
382707UK00001B/118

9 781735 467764